Afrah A. J. is an author exploring the dark side of fiction that thankfully does not reflect her personality as she is certainly not psychotic. She is maybe the only author who never liked reading but took up the most ironic passion of writing. She's a marketing geek with a strong desire to explore the world. A. J. sees herself as a blooming rose in a garden full of authors. Like any sane person, she is also terrified of spiders.

To my wonderful parents, Azra and Jalal, for all the years of support. And of course my partners in crime (please, not literally) Afreen and Afsha, my beautiful sisters who kept me encouraged and went through my book reading, forcefully. And to the most amazing Y - O - U.

Afrah A. J.

MALIGNANCE

AUSTIN MACAULEY PUBLISHERS™

LONDON • CAMBRIDGE • NEW YORK • SHARJAH

ISBN – 9789948806264– (Paperback)
ISBN – 9789948806271– (E-Book)

Application Number: MC-10-01-5941887
Age Classification: 17+

Printer Name: iPrint Global Ltd
Printer Address: Witchford, England

First Published 2023
AUSTIN MACAULEY PUBLISHERS FZE
Sharjah Publishing City
P.O Box [519201]
Sharjah, UAE
www.austinmacauley.ae
+971 655 95 202

Table of Contents

Chapter 1: The Unexpected

The clock had struck eight. It was a blissful morning. She sang along melodiously to the radio. She glanced at her own reflection, giving a sigh of relief for the break she got after solving a few arduous cases along with her team. A 26-year-old woman with beautiful brown eyes had kindness written all over her fair face. Looking through the mirror, she turned her vision toward a faint gunshot wound, on her shoulder.

Proudly, her eyes moved down to look at her identity card. Gracy Brown, deputy superintendent of Annapolis Police Department. She picked it up and passed a satirical smile at her photo. I wasn't even ready, she thought. However, she was proud to be the youngest deputy in her area.

Her room had a queen-sized bed which was always neatly maintained. She was never into designing, which resulted in her effortless room decoration. Every corner of her house smelled like fresh books as she was very fond of reading. As a kid, she always admired mystery and action books, and that is what she turned her life into.

She lived in the beautiful streets of Annapolis, Maryland. It is a small city, and the news about her solving that suspenseful case spread faster than any fire. She was then known by every leaf on the streets.

She sat down and smiled as she admired a picture of her goofing around with the love of her life. The picture was kept in a frame, gifted by the gentleman. A beautiful teal-colored glass with perfectly shaped shells on the borders. Her favorite color and her happy object, he knew her well.

As her brain traveled down the memory lane, a doorbell interrupted her moment. A ring she had been waiting for since the time she planned on getting a vacation, only to spend time with him.

But he's never on time, spoke her inner voice as she rushed downstairs, in her flowy light blue gown. She opened the door that was placed right in front of the last step of her wooden staircase.

'Linette!' It was Gracy's favorite companion.

Linette O'Malley, admired by many due to her shoulder-length, dark brown hair, and the pleasant smile she always carried. Her aura was welcoming. People wondered how she managed to maintain her physical appearance even at her thirty-ninth year of age.

Linette lived with her husband, Aaron. They also had two healthy children. Samantha, her 16-year-old daughter, and Nathan, her 4-year-old son.

'Come on in!' said Gracy, excitedly, as she made way for her to step in. They sat down on her old white Chesterfield sofa that was placed right in front of the fireplace that she never bothered to light up.

'It's been so long, where were you all this while?' asked Linette.

'Work,' She sighed.

'I've heard that excuse before Aaron was out for a week. One week without his family just so he can go to some island. Oh by the way! Made this today.' She stretched her arms toward Gracy and handed her a salver full of pancakes.

Gracy sniffed. 'My fav—Linette you're a savior. Aaron is one lucky man, I tell you.'

'Er, I don't doubt that. He came home tired and disturbed these pancakes better light up his silly mood.'

'Oh, they will.'

'Well, I would have stayed longer but my children might be waiting for their lunch box. I don't want them to bother their father for it.' Linette rushed outside the door.

'We shall catch up soon!' Gracy watched her go to a house, right opposite hers.

Linette went home to find Aaron awake, sitting at the dining table. She struck up random conversations with him as she prepared lunch packets for her children. She continued telling him how much she missed him but he did not seem to show any interest in her impatient words. She walked toward him and gave him a slight nudge, 'you're not listening.'

He gasped. 'But I'm OK. I mean, what? I'm sorry. Honey, of course, I am listening.'

Linette knew something was different about Aaron. From the time he had come home, he wasn't himself. However, she chose to ignore it and continued engaging him in various conversations.

'How was work? What did you do an entire week without my tasty cuisine and my unique love? It was an island, wasn't it? Something Fe—'

'I don't want to go back there,' Aaron whispered as her words triggered his aggression levels.

She leaned toward him and put her hand on his shoulder. 'Aaron?'

Aaron did not hesitate to push her away. 'Get off of me.' He rushed upstairs to his room and slammed the door. She was shocked to witness this moment of tension. Aaron had never behaved insensitively with his family. He always had been that kind of a person who would respect her and the kids no matter how stressed he was.

She was in tears. She rushed upstairs and tenderly knocked on the locked door a few times. She took back her hand when the kids came out of their room.

'Mom is everything OK?' Samantha walked toward her.

Linette nodded a yes and asked her to drop Nathan to his pre-school. Samantha frowned as she held Nathan's hand. 'Guess you are my responsibility today, lil one.' They picked up their lunch box and walked out of the house.

Meanwhile, opposite their house, an opposite situation took place. He was finally at Gracy's doorstep. She looked through the window to find a handsome man standing on the other side of the door with a tulip in his hand. Eric Ainsworth, a tall and polite man. He wore a neatly pressed black and white suit with a strong cologne that struck her nose from the other side of the door. 'He's never worn that before.' She chuckled as her fingers brushed through her hair. She opened the door with a wide grin.

'Ainsworth!' She blushed uncontrollably.

'Mrs. Ainsworth.' He hugged her as tightly as he could.

'I'm still a Brown.'

'Do I smell pancakes?' He strolled toward the appealing smell of, well, pancakes.

'Linette dropped them a few minutes ago.' Gracy unwrapped the foil as the aroma got intense.

'I missed you.' He stuffed his mouth with an entire pancake.

'Missed me or the pancakes?'

'Pancakes, of course.'

They've known each other for almost four years now. Since she was new to Annapolis, she was unaware of the ongoing rumors of a handsome 24-year-old crime scene investigator.

They first met at a crime scene and, believe it or not, hated each other's company. She thought he could use some bookish knowledge about crime whereas he thought well, he thought she needed to smile more often. There wasn't much interaction during the first time, which was a relief from both sides. However, on Gracy's third assignment, she noticed Eric's presence.

'Officer Brown.' He walked past her. She replied to his first words in silence.

Little did they know they were going to have to team up for many more cases. As time passed by, they learned new things about each other that they did not detest. Precisely, on their eleventh case together, they had a real conversation. Gracy lost control over her blush as they started bonding. They finally started to enjoy working as a team and handled them quite impressively.

At Linette's place.

Everything was unexpected. She wanted to know the cause of Aaron's unusual behavior. To end her curiosity, she decided to ring the family members of his team who had gone to the island with him. She saw his phone lying on the ground and took out a list of who all had gone. She called up his close friend, Adrian, but his phone was switched off. She called their landline and a silvery voice picked up.

'Hey Mary, is Adrian home?' Linette asked hastily.

'Linette! Hey, no he is with his team right now.'

'Was he upset or stressed out when he arrived from that island mission?'

Linette had the conversation confused. Mary replied after a reasonable pause, 'My brother's not home yet. Before leaving, he said he'll be back in two or three weeks. I wasn't quite listening.'

There was no response from Linette's side.

'What's wrong?' Mary added.

Linette was startled. 'My bad, see you later!' She hung up and stayed silent as she herself didn't know what was happening.

She dialed Jack's number. His wife, Dianne, received the call. 'Is Jack there?' Her questions started getting impatient.

'Linette? You don't sound so good.'

'I am alright, where is Jack?'

Dianne in absolute unawareness. 'He's out for work. He said he'll be back in around two weeks.'

Linette didn't want to worry anyone so she ignored the topic and claimed that she had called up only to enquire about the details of their work trip. She hung up right away and continued her mini investigation only to find out that no one had returned.

She recalled hiding a spare key to their room, under the rug. She unlocked the door and found the room empty. Aaron was gone. She was pondering to herself helplessly. She wiped tears off of her rosy cheeks and started searching his closet.

'Something?' she whispered to the messy closet as she went through his clothes. A packet of medicine fell down on the floor. She picked it up and read it out loud. 'Oxylintine—depression pills?' A man whose stress ended with one family dinner had started looking for peace in some pills?

'Something might have really pushed you to a point to take these. What are you hiding from me?' She started imagining all the wrong scenarios—was he cheating on her? Did something happen on that Island? Did he get fired?

Meanwhile, Gracy and Eric were getting into his car until he rushed back inside to get his blazer.

'This is important.' He rushed back outside and took over the steering wheel.

'Blazer's important? Since when?' Gracy frowned while putting on the seat belt.

'Let's go!' Eric exclaimed excitedly.

Gracy laughed. 'Last time you were this excited you asked me out.'

Eric responded with a grin.

He took the car to Gracy's favorite restaurant. 'Mr. and Mrs. Ainsworth?' Eric asked the person behind the registration desk.

'Yes, please follow me,' said the receptionist, walking toward two empty chairs. They followed her high-heeled black Louis Vuitton that elegantly tapped against the wooden flooring. The food place had an ambiance to die for. The soft clamoring of the forks and the knives against the glass plates, and the faint redolence of roasted chicken mixed with that of the lake water made Gracy feel calm.

She looked at Eric with a mysterious smile. They sat down on the side of the restaurant with a soft breeze touching their souls. Just as Gracy was about to start a conversation, she noticed her favorite song in the background. 'I'm sensing—'

'Yeah, but what's that behind you?' Eric pointed out an absolutely empty lake.

She turned back. 'What's what?' And looked back at Eric.

To her surprise, he was on his knees, holding a square-cut ruby ring. His hands were confident and firm, just like the question he was about to pop.

'Gracy Brown, will you marry me?' He gazed at her shoulder-length, brunette hair that smoothly kissed her face. 'Hey, you look beautiful from this angle as well.'

'I have to be dreaming, right?'

'No, cause the song's about to get over and my knees hurt.'

'Oh!' She laughed. 'Of course! Is that even a question? I will marry you!' She leveled her body to that of his and hugged him with all her heart.

'Watch the ring!' They chuckled as he gently slipped the ring through her finger. 'You make it look so beautiful,' he admired.

'This was unexpected—can't believe you went with a cliché proposal!' They sat back on the chairs as the beautiful bride blushed.

'She said yes!' Eric exclaimed with a childish big smile on his face as the crowd cheered and wooed in joy. For them, nothing could go wrong that day.

On the other hand, Linette went to Gracy's for help but no one answered the door. She was left alone with the thoughts of losing Aaron to the world. Everything went wrong for her that day. She went back home and found her kids on the table, patiently waiting for lunch.

'Papa?' asked Nathan. Linette had no answer to that. Samantha knew something was unusual in the house.

'Mom, what is happening?' She kept her question hushed as Nathan stared at them.

Linette did not want to worry her children. 'Father's at work,' she lied. 'Work' she whispered and realized that she had one last call to make. She rushed to her room and called Aaron's office.

'Alfred Research Center, how can I help you?' asked a thick Missouri accent through the phone.

'Is Aaron O'Malley there?' she asked.

'He has gone out for work.'

'Well then put Stefano on line!'

'Please stay patient while I connect your call to Stefano Alfred's office.' Her calm fingers waited for a while before connecting the call, thinking if she was allowed to connect the call or not. However, she needed reasons to burden her boss and finally, connected the call.

'I told you I do not want to receive calls today!' Stefano yelled from his office, hoping for her to stop bothering him someday. 'What?' he yelled to the caller.

Linette calmly replied, 'I am so sorry to disturb you I'm Linette, Aaron's wife, do you remem—'

'Linette! How can I forget that sweet voice! What can I do for you?' he interrupted.

'You sent some people on that Island along with my husband, none of them are back!' She started freaking out.

'No worries, I told them it'll take two to three weeks for this and it's only been a week and a half.' His voice took an obvious tone.

Linette knew he was unaware of the situation and said, 'You don't get it, Aaron is back and he—'

'Wait, what? Are you sure he's back? Maybe you saw someone else—'

'I think I'd know if I saw my husband in my house sleeping beside me.'

'They weren't supposed to be back so soon'

'No one else came back, only Aaron did and now he's missing too! He wasn't himself in the morning. You have to inform the police!' She panicked.

Stefano needed time to process her information. 'Slow down. What do you mean no one came back? Aaron was with them, there's no way—'

'My husband came back from work disturbed and stressed out. I called up the others to check on them but their families said they weren't home. No one's home'

'Linette, I will look into this matter right away. Please take care of your—' She hung up before he could say more.

'How is this even possible? Martha!' He called his assistant and asked her to call up everyone who had gone for the research. After a while, she came back to his office and informed him that all of their phones were unreachable. Even the ferry master confirmed that their ship was never anchored back to the dock.

'I am not sure if Linette is speaking the truth but if Aaron really did come back home and others didn't make it, we have to inform the police.' Following this statement, Alfred called up the Annapolis Police Department and gave them intel about the current situation.

Moments later, the team had arrived at their office. The case was assigned to Gracy's team. They voted on scattering around the town and interrogating each researcher's family. All of them said the same thing, ' He told me he had to go to an Island for some work and that he would be back within two or three weeks.'

However, Linette had something else to say. 'He came back! He was disturbed and he is a nice person, but he pushed me away when I tried asking him about his unusual behavior.' Linette went breathless.

'Are you sure it was your husband?' Jacob, one of Gracy's promising and narcissistic team members, raised his eyebrows and pressed his lips.

'Why does everyone keep asking me that?'

The team had their doubts about Aaron. None of the members came back home except for him. He was disturbed and stressed out. He was nowhere to be found. These were clear symptoms of a murderer.

'Ma'am, did Aaron have personal grudges against any of these people?' Poppy, Gracy's most practical team member, questioned.

'No, they were all good friends, I'd rather say family,' said Linette in a soft voice.

Jacob passed a suspicious look. 'Was he an aggressive person? Does he get violent with anyone who gets him furious?'

After these questions, Linette realized that they were blaming Aaron for something he certainly did not do.

'No!' she yelled. 'He is a good person, officer. He handles every tough situation with calm—'

'But you said he pushed you away this morning. Don't cover up for your husband, he might be something you don't know.'

Poppy eyed Jacob, indirectly asking him to shut his trap.

Linette had nothing else to utter, she knew the police were looking at this from a wrong angle. She wanted to believe that her husband was completely innocent.

'Thank you for your time. If Aaron comes back home, call us immediately.' Poppy warned as they left the house.

After the interrogation, Poppy collected all the members' images and went to Marcos Morales, the most attentive member of the team, who had the list of information that consisted of all researchers' names and statements from their families. 'William, Gale, Jack, Adrian, Akshay, Ryan, Evan, Aaron,' he said while going through the images.

'What about Roger?' Poppy added.

About that,' Sophia, a new member of the team, added. 'His phone was switched off and there was no one at his place. I didn't know what to do.'

'Newbies, am I right?' Jacob scoffed.

'You should have gone with her,' Poppy whispered.

Sophia ignored the mock and continued, 'I asked Stefano about him. He said Roger had no one. His parents died when he was eighteen years old and was on his own after that. He died without a family.'

Marcos looked at Sophia. 'Died? Who said he died? Who said anyone died?'

They all looked at each other as Poppy interrupted the dubious room. 'What if this isn't murder? What if we're interpreting this situation wrong?'

Chapter 2: A Mysterious Massacre

It was night, the environment at Linette's place was soundless until a doorbell broke her impatient wait. She opened the door to find Aaron on the other side. She pulled him inside and bombarded him with questions. 'The police started questioning your morals! What happened on that island? Answer me now!'

Aaron stared at her steadily. Without uttering a word, he looked at the empty hallway and started walking toward it. She was done with his ignorance. She held his hand and clenched his skin while investing all her strength. He looked into her eyes and snarled inhumanly. To her horror, his eyes were almost bloodshot. She left his hand and slowly took a few steps back as he walked toward her. Those eyes did not possess Aaron's charm anymore. It was something else, something callous. Linette knew she wasn't looking at her husband.

He wrapped his hand around her neck and firmed his grip. 'Aaron!' She choked and tried her best to come out of the lock.

Samantha and Nathan came running downstairs and found their father strangling their mother.

'Nathan, go back to your room!' Samantha yelled as she held Aaron from behind. Showing no mercy, Aaron pushed her to the ground and continued to apply more pressure on Linette's neck. His clear aim was to kill her.

'Gracy.' Linette's voice broke as she tried to free herself. Samantha rushed outside toward Gracy's house and started banging on her door with scared fists. 'Grace!' she cried. No one was home. The entire neighborhood was sleeping. Her cry for help wasn't loud enough.

The newly engaged couple were almost home with wide smiles on their faces, that is until they saw Samantha banging on the door, bursting into heavy tears. Their smiles disappeared as they got out of the car.

'Samantha?' Gracy rushed toward the broken soul. Eric heard Nathan's cry and walked toward the shriek.

'He's trying to kill her!' Samantha cried.

Eric followed her words and sprinted. He put a sudden brake on his leg when he found Linette on the floor. A blurry vision of a man escaping is all he got while trying to chase him down. 'Stop!' Confused between chasing the man and helping Linette, he chose the latter.

He hurried back inside to find Linette's motionless body lying on the floor. At that very moment, he only wished he wasn't looking at a dead body. He knelt down to check her pulse, while staring at Nathan's wrinkled face, almost crushing his stuffed toy in fear. Time froze at that very moment. Eric's eye flickered as he tried his best to find a pulse.

After a long pause, he gave a sigh of relief as he felt a faint vibration. 'She's fine. Mommy's just napping.' The child was too naive to believe in his words. He lifted Linette and walked outside as he watched Nathan run to his sister.

'Where's your father?' asked Gracy.

'He was the one trying to hurt her,' Samantha whispered while covering Nathan's pure ears. Gracy was appalled, she refused to believe what she had heard. But Samantha loved her father too much to portray him as the culprit.

'Is she alright?' Samantha asked Eric as he brought her inside.

'She just needs a little rest.' He comfortably placed her body on the sofa.

At Annapolis Police Department.

'Do we know where the crew members are?' Zachery, the inquisitive member of the team, asked.

'They're all missing. Although the captain of the ship, Bligh Thomas, his neighbor said that he saw him come back home and then leave immediately with packed bags,' Marcos replied.

'Ah! So the ship did anchor itself at the dock.' Sophia raised his eyebrows.

'Brilliant observation,' Jacob mocked.

'The neighbors confirmed Aaron's presence?' Poppy joined the conversation.

'They did,' Alexis Morales, a calm team member, Marcos' younger brother, replied with a sigh of frustration. They interrogated everyone in the office and found no reason to hold Aaron as a suspect.

'Aaron knows something very important.' Zachery squinted his eyes at Aaron's image, hoping for it to speak up.

At Gracy's place.

She pulled Eric aside and lowered her voice. 'Did you see him do it?'

'That man fled away the moment he felt my presence—'

'It was Aaron.' She looked at Linette's quiet body.

Eric was startled. 'Her own husband?'

'Why did he do this?' Samantha interrupted.

'I don't know what happened back at the house. Your father doesn't seem to be in his right mind.' Gracy looked into Samantha's hurting eyes.

'He loves us, you know? I knew something was wrong with him but we all were so ignorant. Please save him from himself.' Samantha stood there, trying to figure out what went wrong.

'Mommy!' Nathan squealed as Linette stressfully opened her eyes. They gathered around her and chose to stay silent. Linette was traumatized. She could feel her husband's hands tightly gripping around her neck. Her eyes felt as if they were going to pop out any minute.

'Kids, are you OK?' she asked with absolutely no expression on her face. She was physically there but mentally in the past, recalling how her husband tried strangling her as his eyes went completely blood-shot in the process. He, who never even raised his voice in front of his family, tried to kill his wife. They took her upstairs to the bedroom to recover from the incident. But will she ever recover from it?

Gracy was about to speak to Linette until two police cars pulled up nearby. She ran downstairs to find her team standing outside Linette's house.

'Officers!' She opened the door and called them out.

There's always one all-rounder member in a team, a person who even their leader looks up to them. Hunter Callahan. Imagine almost all good qualities in an officer, that's him. Imagine all the bad qualities in a man, that's not him.

'We got a case from this house!' Hunter yelled across the street.

Already? She thought. 'Come here. There's no one in that house,' she yelled back.

Jacob and Hunter entered Gracy's house and explained everything from the start, about them going to Aaron's office, about the suspects and the interrogations that took place. Normally, Gracy would've been disappointed in herself for being absent throughout the process, but she deserved a moment with Eric.

'So all of you are here to see if Aaron came back home?' Gracy asked.

'Nah. Only Hunter and I are here for that. The others are here for the two murder reports that took place near this street,' Jacob casually stated.

'Murder reports, you say?' Gracy frowned. She hoped that Aaron fleeing away after attacking his wife and that the murder reports were nothing but just a coincidence. 'Aaron—he tried killing his wife half an hour ago,' she added as she pinched her forehead.

After a pause, Jacob said, 'I already had a bad feeling about this man. Do you think he murdered—'

'Stop that!' Linette yelled as she padded downstairs. 'He would never kill anyone. Look, I'm alive! I faintly remember him apologizing to me before running away. He said something about him not being in his complete senses and that something else is taking control over his body and that he didn't mean for any of it to happen.'

Jacob in annoyance, 'Ah, Grace I think whoever in our lockup apologizes for what they did should be set free. Covering up for that man.'

'You don't understand. I have been staying with "that man" for years! I know him!' Linette cried. 'Gracy, you know him too, help me out here.'

'I know.' Gracy looked down. 'I do know him, he would never do wrong to anyone. I hope it wasn't him.' Gracy did not want to believe that it was Aaron. Her role of being a friend and a police officer clashed. She did not know which one to pick. For the first time, Gracy found herself in a personal-professional clashing dilemma.

As the conversation ended, the others walked in. 'It's not there. It was probably a hoax. People try to take advantage of our fast service—' Poppy started ranting.

'Hoax?' Gracy asked.

'Someone texted us these pictures of two dead bodies. I must say they're very disturbing images. It was anyway too gross to be true. The person messaged, "Come and get them before it is too late." There was nothing. I don't see any dead bodies around this area,' Marcos replied.

'Show me those pictures.' Gracy put her hand forward. Poppy placed the printed images over her curious palm. Gracy was disgusted at the first glimpse. Their faces were unidentifiable. It was as if something had chewed off their faces until the skull was revealed. Their blood-shot eyes were pushed inside and were partially squished.

'You're right, it is too gross to be true. That's photoshop right there, but to be on the safer side, run these through forensics. Also messing with police officers, huh? Find this person.'

Meanwhile, Dr. Collins rang Eric's phone.

Dr. Charles Collins. A hard-working pathologist who loved his wife and his 20-year-old son who always took a keen interest in his father's work. His fifty years of age spoke for his experience in the field.

He owned a morgue that was connected to Collins' Research Center, a rival of Alfred's. The center was owned by his younger sister, Katherine Collins, a virologist. It was their dream to set up a Morgue and a research center, along with a side clinic. Their center was more than active at the moment as many dead bodies knocked on their door. Those cases were something they swore they had never seen before.

Dr. Collins rang Eric's phone to give him some interesting facts about John Doe he had been working on. 'Eric, this one's different. Looks like the body was a meal to something. The forensic reports are a blur. We still don't know the cause of his death. His blood is unusually very dark and thick; it's almost like jelly.'

'No signs of strangling? No poison?' asked Eric.

'Just a bite,' Charles replied.

'A bite could either be a coyote or a cannibal!' Eric nodded as he realized the situation was not to be made fun of. 'Weird things are happening today, doctor.'

'It's a massacre out there. I'm worried it could be a horrible virus.'

'That one body is a massacre for you?' Eric scoffed.

'One body? Eric, are you not aware of what's happening?' Charles put down the test tube that contained John Doe's blood.

Eric, after a pause, questioned, 'I am not aware of what exactly?'

Charles wanted to answer all his questions but something unusual in the blood sample caught his attention. He picked up the test tube between his fingers to take a closer look. To his surprise, he could see small yellow parasites that were almost visible with his bare eyes. It seemed as if they were all combining together and acting up aggressively.

'How did I miss this?' Charles whispered to himself.

'Dr. Collins?'

'I'm sorry. Eric, there were five dead bodies near this area and none of them died pretty. All these bodies are unknown, just can't seem to identify them.'

'Did I hear you right? Five dead bodies, you said?'

Charles's wrinkled forehead, he had no idea what he was looking at. He turned back to examine the blood sample but found himself in a gruesome scene. The test tube fell out of his fingers as it reached a boiling point. 'No way.'

'Dr. Charles?' On getting no reply, Eric yelled into the microphone, 'Dr. Charles!' All Eric could hear were distorted screams.

'Eric, help! Jo—'

But it was too late. The call got disconnected. Eric Ainsworth was left in absolute horror. Wasting no time, he asked Alexis and Marcos to go with him to the center.

'What's wrong?' Gracy asked as she watched him hurry.

Eric didn't know if he had time to pause his feet and explain. After blankly staring at her anxious face, he chose not to worry her. 'Just checking up on Dr. Charles, Be safe, OK?' He kissed her frown and rushed out of the house with the Morales brothers.

On their way to the center, Eric tried calling Charles but it went straight to voicemail. The entire ride was him staring at his phone for a call back, but it never rang.

Back at Gracy's place.

Gracy and her teammates visited the neighborhood to ask if they had noticed anything unusual around them. Whereas Sophia and Hunter volunteered to stay back at Gracy's to look after Linette and her children.

During the investigation, surprisingly, all their children had a uniform answer, 'I saw Uncle Aaron eat a human.' But the parents confirmed it as a silly hoax.

'They said the same thing last month about my husband. They always prank around. My apologies to you, they're only kids,' said one of the parents.

Not considering the statements given by the children, they stopped the investigation. They ended up gathering no information, which made it difficult for them to proceed with any kind of assumptions.

'We need to know where Roger is,' said Gracy.

'We could break into his house look, for clues,' Jacob added as he handed over a search warrant to Gracy.

'Then why are we still here? Let's go.'

'Poppy, stay here.' Jacob and the others rushed into the car as she looked at him furiously. He never included her, Poppy wondered why. She sat at Gracy's doorstep and watched them leave.

While hitting the accelerator, Gracy turned on the radio only to find out that the city was facing an apocalypse. Along with death reports, a large number of missing reports had been lodged and it did not look like they were decreasing anytime soon. All the police branches were active at the moment.

'What's going on?' She whispered.

At Collin 's Research Center.

Eric and his brothers rushed toward the morgue through a long passage. On reaching Charles's workplace, they found the room's door to be wide open.

'Dr. Collins?' Eric called out hesitantly as he peeped inside the morgue. It was empty. There were no bodies on the bed either. All they could see were broken glasses, shattered test tubes, and blood splattered all over the floor. It seemed as if they had entered a slaughterhouse.

'Is that a—'

'Heart,' Eric completed Alexis' trepidation. This made them retch. Eric gasped as he stepped on a broken phone lying on the ground. 'The morgue's meters away from the center. No one else could've heard him scream. We need to know what happened here.'

A camera caught Marcos's eyes. 'Where's the control room?'

'It's in the center,' Eric replied in a dull voice.

Little did they know what they were about to encounter there.

Inside Gracy's car.

Gracy and the others were horror-struck after listening to what was happening around them. As they were on their way to Roger's, they came across speeding police cars and ambulances. All of them were going in different directions.

'What kind of an apocalypse is this?' Zachery whispered to himself. 'Those are the SWAT sirens. Heard those tires only once in my practical exam.'

'That one. Pull over.' Jacob pointed out a house after rolling his eyes at Zachery's panic.

It was an old bungalow that appeared to be low-spirited. It had broken windows and a creaking gate.

'He's home?' Gracy frowned. The door was unlocked and voices of the foot against the wooden floorings were heard. Gracy rang the doorbell once but got no response.

'Open up or else we'll do it ourselves!' Jacob yelled.

After that harsh warning, a man around forty years of age with a disturbed face opened the door.

'What?' asked the man.

'Roger?' Gracy stepped forward.

'Yes, you're here at an ungodly hour, why?'

'APD. Let us in.' They flipped their identity cards and leveled the warrant to his vision.

Roger's face went pale. He apologized and stepped aside for them to enter. His house was filthy as if he never bothered to maintain it. A mild fragrance of lavender was circulating in the environment. The fireplace was left untouched. The curtains were always drawn. The house made him look like someone who had nothing to lose and hence, the effortless cleaning of the house.

Roger offered them some water and seemed casual about the police wandering around his house at midnight.

Gracy frowned at his calmness. 'Roger Thomas, the police are looking for you.'

He stopped pouring the water and sighed. 'Well then, officer, you've found me.' He carefully placed the glass in front of them.

'Take a seat.' She played along.

Roger sat down, still very calm, pretending as if nothing had happened. 'Um, did I do something?' But he was already aware of the reason.

Jacob looked at him and scoffed. 'You don't know? What happened on that island, Roger?'

Roger turned his face in another direction, away from the officers, as if he was trying to look away from reality. He chose silence.

'It seems no one has come back to Annapolis after the trip except for you and Aaron,' Gracy raised her voice.

'I don't want to justify myself,' Roger's voice was barely audible. He had given up on the real story. It was something no one would ever believe in. He knew it was over for him. 'Just put me in jail or whatever! You wouldn't even consider my story.' He turned to Gracy.

'Try us.' Gracy leaned forward, lending her ears.

'Everyone's in danger,' Roger whispered while fidgeting with his hands. A bubble of nervousness started building around him, and he wasn't ready to pop it.

The tensive silence broke as Jacob's phone buzzed. He stepped outside to receive.

'Roger, if I were you, I'd spill it out. We're listening.' Gracy sympathized.

'Officers.' Jacob barged inside the house. 'Four murder reports in under five minutes, can you imagine?'

They've never experienced multiple and unexplained cases like this before. They were dealing with an unknown cause, and no one could explain this better than the man sitting in front of them.

'You do know something about this, don't you?' Zachery observed Roger's panic.

Roger's regretful voice took over. 'I do.'

Chapter 3: Unrevealed Island

"I remember every moment of that day for it had changed our lives for the worse. Like every other day, Aaron, William, Evan, Jack, Akshay, Adrian, Ryan, Gale, and I were sitting together in the canteen during the lunch hour. We were a definition of a true team, always worked and spent leisure time together. None of us ever let any kind of personal grudges tarnish the bond we had built over the years. They were my only true family.

That day, Stefano's assistant Martha came to us and we got called to an urgent meeting.

'Hello, boys, what are you all up to today?'

Everyone exclaimed, 'Hey, Martha!'

'Boss just received an interesting assignment from the government for you all,' Martha added.

'What is it, Martha?' Akshay asked.

'Oh dear, there is a meeting in an hour. Mr. Alfred will be giving you the details then. I want you all to freshen up and meet me at the top floor conference room.'

'Top floor?' Gale asked.

'But the top floor is for confidential meetings. Is someone else going to be joining us today?' Ryan asked.

Martha paused and sighed. 'Yes, someone important will be there. I'm sorry boys, I'm not authorized to reveal any more information. Dress pretty!'

Martha exited the room leaving us clueless. We had never been to the top floor before.

William passed a perplexed look to everyone and added, 'That was strange. Let's get ready.'

We all slipped into our tuxedos. It surely seemed like we were on a mission, before even knowing it. A mission that we probably weren't prepared for. We were never assigned by the government before. So, we were all stiff but there was a tinge of excitement. We entered the elevator. The building had fifty floors and we had to get to the top.

Akshay pressed the top floor button with confidence. 'I got to press the button without the promotion!'

Akshay tried lightening up the mood so that the tension in the air broke. Everyone surely did laugh, but still, the air couldn't be changed.

The elevator door opened to the finest carpet laid all around the office floor, cold and bright lights all over. Martha was sitting in her office and noticed us walking toward the conference room. She rushed toward us, asked us to stay patient, and settled us down on a beautiful red sofa. The top floor had a different and a new aroma. We had never seen that part of the office; it was so luxurious, I remember. Everyone wandered and admired the place like a child until Martha asked us to gather around.

I apologize for my very specific storytelling; I have to relive every single moment of it. I'm also afraid to jump to the fatal part.

'I know this is a big thing for you all but you cannot just loiter around in here. The meeting starts in a minute, try not to look too excited. The President needs serious faces for this assignment,' she said.

'The who?' Gale yelled in a high-pitched tone as he looked at everyone with a grin. Everyone's jaw dropped; they were speechless.

'Boys, please lose that face and follow me,' said Martha as she walked toward the conference room.

She told us that the meeting was with the President. Boy, were we shocked to hear that. We entered the room and saw the man. It was such an honor for us to be in the same room as him. He obviously is a busy man, what made the meeting so important that he had to be present for it, you ask? I'll get to that part soon.

For the first few minutes, we did not believe that our President was right in front of us. I don't think any of us concentrated on Stefano's words; we just wanted the President to take over. And then he finally did.

He spoke about an island… Fenjiyawa island. An island that was unknown to all, never heard of. They wanted to know if the island was fit for building a secret nuclear weapon. He had a few confidential papers in one file with him that he wouldn't disclose. Now that I look back, I think my boss and he had some sort of a deal and were onto something big.

Anyway, us being the top researchers they came to us. It seemed questionable, but there was no way to deny a direct offer from the President—maybe that's why he wanted to be present during the agenda discussion. Well, I don't think it was an offer, more of an order. We weren't allowed to talk about this to anyone… protocol.

The place seemed tricky; it was in the middle of nowhere—the Pacific Ocean to be a little more precise. We didn't even know how they found the island in the first place.

We were expected to explore the entire island and report back in three weeks. They didn't know how much time it would take for us to reach there. It was all on us, they didn't know jack shit!

But of course, we weren't suspicious about anything and took this mission lightly. Now that I look back in time, we could've refused this mission.

Anyway, they asked us to leave in two days so they arranged a ship and we left the continent.

'It feels good to be out here with my only family,' said Roger as he sobbed.

Everyone looked at him and raised their glass of wine. 'To us!' they exclaimed.

'I mean I adore you guys, but I already miss my wife and my baby girl,' said Gale.

'Hey, isn't she turning one year old next month?' Akshay asked.

'Yes, she is. That's the reason I did not deny this project. With that unimaginable pay we're getting to do this… we can celebrate our girl's birthday somewhere big.'

'And we're invited!' Aaron exclaimed.

'Not to sound cheesy or anything but you boys are honestly everything I have and—' Roger's voice started to mumble as he emptied a bottle of rose wine.

'Being drunk, you are so emotional I love it.' Jack laughed.

'Wow! Boss is going to kill us if he finds out that we were drinking on the ship, going for a mission, for the President,' added William as realization kicked in.

'Lay back and drink more! No one is going to complain. Until someone does,' added Aaron.

'I might! I could use any kind of promotion right now.' Akshay smirked.

'You lil sneak!' Ryan shrieked.

'Guys, guess who I am? Hi you all!' Evan mimicked Martha.

'Give her a break! She doesn't talk like that.' Ryan mumbled.

'Oh shut up you! Why don't you just tell her that you like her?' Gale poured himself another glass of wine.

'Look at me. She's got a thing for you, and everyone knows that. Tell her you like her, you tell her that.' Roger extended his arm for Gale to pour more wine into his glass.

'I promise that the moment we go back home, I will ask her out.' Ryan blushed.

'That's my man!' Jack exclaimed.

'Now, sleep! Fenjiyawa's a blink away,' Aaron exaggerated.

'Goodnight you all!' Adrian mocked as everyone laughed hard.

'Shut up!' Ryan nodded and closed his eyes.

It took us approximately five days to reach Fenjiyawa. The crew members anchored our ship and we all climbed down. It was an old, abandoned island. It wasn't one of those aesthetic ones—the grass was dried up and a storm was about to take over. It felt like mother nature was trying to warn us about something. Ignoring the signals, we stepped into the woods. Fenjiyawa seemed like a complete waste but we still kept our hopes alive and did go on. A few minutes later, we heard noises. They weren't clear. No one was worried as such. In fact, everyone had their mesmerized faces on.

We followed the noise and went toward the denser part of the island.

'Maybe we should go back, I don't have a good feeling about this,' Ryan's voice shivered.

'You want to turn down the project our President gave?' Jack asked rhetorically.

'You want to turn your back on the promotion we might get?' Added Gale.

'Wait, I have one that will really make you think! You want to go back after coming all the way here?' Asked Roger.

'I mean, the way you guys are putting it, no! Obviously not,' Ryan stuttered.

'That's what I thought,' said everyone in unison.

After walking a little further, we saw empty bamboo cages. It was as if something had escaped from it. As our vision looked beyond these cages, there were more and they had people in them, diseased people. They were very sick.

We thought they were probably caged by tribals, a lot of islands usually have those. Now, we didn't want to get ourselves into any trouble, so we decided to leave. But Gale and William! They had this human decency, you see? They both started opening the cages until we realized that they shouldn't have. They made a mistake.

These diseased people turned toward us. Their eyes were all white, I could see thick red blood clots all over their bodies and we could tell that they weren't friendly. You must think why we didn't see that before opening the cages. But officers, at times like this, you never focus on the problem, you focus on solving them. But weirdly! There was more coming from everywhere!

I couldn't move. None of us could. Everyone's feet froze. William was able to run away from them but when Jack tried taking a step back, one of the diseased men grabbed his neck and peeled off his skin with his rotten teeth. My man turned around, looked at us, and grabbed his bleeding neck. It didn't help him much with the bleeding.

I could see fear in his eyes. Last time I saw fear in those eyes was… never. On that island, at that very moment, he knew he wasn't going to make it. I saw him fall to the ground as another diseased human started eating off his right foot—details.

'Jackie!' Gale yelled as he made a head start toward the ship.

Blood poured out of Jack's mouth, he weakly signaled them to leave the island by pointing at the ship. A voice came from the back of his dying throat, 'Go.'

'No!' Evan cried out loud as he saw more diseased people walking toward them.

In a matter of seconds, we lost Jack and we couldn't do anything. Don't take us for being insensitive, leaving our friend behind. The first time you officers saw a crime taking place, I bet you froze. All we did was scream. We cried for help. There were no sane people left around. More of their kind emerged out of the woods. We did not want to leave Jack behind, but we were left with no other choice. They were eating him up like animals like barbarians! We ran toward our ship, we ran for our lives, we just ran.

'Guys, catch up!' Roger yelled.
Ryan yelled as he was pounced upon by dozens of the infected ones.
'Ryan!!!' Adrain cried out loud.
'What the hell is happening?' Aaron yelled at Roger as they rushed toward the ship.

"What the hell is happening?" How would I have a reply for that? One by one we lost the entire group! I looked behind while running and watched my family vanish into the woods. Fenjiyawa snatched them away.

Adrian, Aaron, and I were lucky enough to outrun them. We boarded the ship and tried explaining this to the crew members. We were scared, we were angry, and we did not know what to do. At one point, I think I even started speaking Gibberish. They weren't ready to listen and didn't want to go back without all the researchers on board. Who else was going to board? Everyone was dead! I remember this one stubborn captain, Bligh Thomas, he just wouldn't lend his ears.

They started believing us when they heard growling noises. Our impatience increased when these haunting voices got closer. They used their binoculars and were horrified to see the island's face. It was an "I told you so" moment for us.

We had to sail off as soon as possible, and we did. Something they saw on the island convinced them to leave the land right away.

I don't know what to say, officers. I lost everything. We were traumatized. Three of us sat down on the edge of the ship.

'What was that?' Adrian blankly stared at the sky.
'Do you think anyone made it?' Roger shivered.
'No, I saw their bodies on the ground. I don't get it.' Terror had engulfed them.
'Gale was—he was supposed to go back home and meet his family—his wife, his daughter. What?' Aaron looked at Roger, not quite hoping for a response.

I wish I had the answers.

The island started getting smaller. It came to my notice that none of the crew members or the captain had come to us to talk about it. Maybe we weren't looking so appealing, or maybe they were just doing their job. You know, I've always been an optimist, lost my family, and lost a lot of jobs too, but I never gave up. The universe gets a little jealous sometimes of how strong we are and throws a pile of tragedy on our faces.

The moment we thought we were getting away from a disaster, Adrian started complaining about a throbbing pain. He was bit by our dear old friend… surprise.

We panicked when he started rambling some horrible things. Now, I know who they are and what each one of them would say in certain situations. When Adrian started speaking, it was as if someone else controlled his words.

'What if I turn into one of those things?' Adrian panicked.

'I'm sure you'll be fine, OK?' Aaron assured.

'Aaron, I saw them turn! You didn't!'

'Adrian, panicking will make it worse, you will be fine!' Roger added.

'Easy for you to say, you don't have a family to go back to.' Adrian scoffed without hesitation. 'I have one and they need me!'

'What did you say?' Roger asked rhetorically.

'You heard me right. People around you end up dead! And now, more than half of us are gone and it's all because of you!' Adrian stomped away.

'Don't listen to him, he's losing his mind.'

Aaron calmed me down. I guess at that point I lost Adrian too. Well, that man wanted to be left alone so we let him be.

The island was nothing but a dot, Fenjiyawa was long gone. We dozed off on the dock. The next morning, screams woke us up.

'Get off of me, you sick man!' yelled one of the crew members.

'Sir! Unhand my fellow!' The captain of the ship came out of his cabin.

We ran toward the chaos and saw Adrian attacking one of the crew members as others tried pulling him away. He did not look sick; he was just aggressive.

Next thing we know, we joined the tiff and Aaron pushed Adrian off of the ship, by mistake. It was a mistake. Everything got quiet after a water splash, I couldn't process anything. Do you know those high-frequency noises that take over the ambiance? I heard those while watching him drown in the water as he called out my name and cried for help. I fell for those words.

'Adrian! Adrian! Hold on, I got you brother!' Roger blindly threw a rope into the water.

'Roger! Aaro—' Adrian disappeared into the water.

'What did you do?!' Roger looked at Aaron as he started hyperventilating.

I threw him a rope but his scared hands couldn't seem to grab a hold of it. Aaron told me that it was the right thing to do. Yeah, I'm sure it wasn't easy for him either. Everything happened in seconds, I don't know how to explain it. I didn't think I'd be able to actually sit here and recall all those incidents. Losing my family, again, kills me from the inside. I've lost hope. I've given up. You win, universe.

Now Aaron showed me a scratch on his arm too, and it was pretty deep alright. He got it from Adrian. We didn't panic this time. You need energy to panic, it was all flushed out. We waited, but nothing really happened so we thought we were safe.

On reaching Annapolis, we planned on keeping our mouths shut about this till we figured out a way to—yeah, we were going to cook up a story. I guess we just wanted to stay out of the suspect zone. I knew this day was coming, OK? A lot of researchers went missing and this mission was huge. It wouldn't have gone unnoticed. We just needed more time for the incident to seep in.

I met Aaron this morning, and he said that he felt as if something was controlling him—something was rushing in his blood and that made him feel uncomfortable. At least that's what he told me. But then we had an argument and he stormed out of my house. I don't—I'm not sure what happened after that."

'Roger, how do we know you aren't making this up? Is there any evidence to support your case? Alibis to confirm your meeting with Aaron?' Gracy questioned as the other two officers were speechless.

'I told you already, he was at my home—no alibis, officer. Listen, I wish this was made up, and I'm glad I don't have any evidence from that day.' Roger inhaled sharply and tried holding back his tears.

Aaron's unusual behavior, him attacking Linette and the kids, children saying that they saw Aaron attack a person, and the unexplained murder reports. Gracy had connected all the dots. Roger's story started making sense.

'Did he just rant out a zombie movie plot? With a straight face throughout?' Zachery whispered to Jacob. He did not buy the story whatsoever.

'I don't think Eric is safe.' Gracy stood up. 'Don't leave the city. We'll come back for you again.'

The officers rushed outside the house as they left Roger in torment. His muscles strained as his fingers and toes twitched. His brain kept reminding him of how his friends screamed and begged for life. He looked up at his flask, containing rum. He had sworn to his friends that it would stay untouched. Watching the still flask through his blurred eyes made him realize that he had no one to stop him from gulping it down.

At the Collin's Research Center.

'There. That's the footage.' Eric pointed out one of the screens.

'And that's our John Doe,' Alexis focused.

Their eyes started drying up as nothing suspicious took place in the first few minutes. Charles was just doing his job whereas John Doe was doing his job by lying dead on the table. They forwarded the footage to the point where Charles started a conversation with Eric. They saw him looking at a test tube very closely—as if saw something with his bare eyes.

'Wait, rewind?' Marcos was moved. 'John Doe winced.'

Ignoring his words, Eric nodded. 'Marcos, he's cut open. It's probably just a glitch.'

After a while, the video had reached the point where it all began. Charles turned around to find John Doe alive. Clearly, this was no glitch. The body sat up straight as his organs plunged to the ground. It's rare when a doctor is unhappy to see a man alive. 'Eric! Help! John Doe is alive!' Not realizing the disconnected call, he kept yelling for help and hoped that Eric would save him somehow.

All six scared eyes were locked on the screen. Their bodies were so stationary that they felt their hearts pumping faster as fresh blood rushed through their veins. Terror replaced the air as they witnessed John Doe tear off Charles's flesh. He was not human. A Cannibal? A Zombie? A Vampire? Doesn't matter, Charles was its meal.

'What is that?' Marcos gulped. Of course, no one had an answer to that.

They saw John Doe leave the room, leaving Charles's dead body in complete isolation. They did not want to look at the screen anymore, however, they couldn't seem to take their eyes off it either.

A few minutes later, Charles woke up from death and behaved differently.

'Wait, now he's awake too?' Alexis took a few steps back as if Charles would reach out to him through the screen.

The doctor had John Doe's lungs for dinner. His mouth was filled with blood and not once did he feel disgusted about it. His face did not wrinkle, he seemed very unhesitant about gobbling down another corpse's organs. The details weren't clear in the footage but one thing was—the center was no longer safe.

'Charles and John Doe, they're still out here.' Alexis let in air through mouth.

'Until his last breath, all he said was "Eric help" and I wasn't there.' Eric was disturbed after witnessing Charles's miserable death and him coming back to life.

'Eric, we need to evacuate the area.' Alexis placed his hand on Eric's shoulder.

'I know.' Eric looked down while leaving the room, only to bump into a body.

'Sorry,' he muttered. The reply was aggressive, the man opposite him held his shoulders with a tight grip. A sudden jerk of movement hit his consciousness as he lifted his fatigue face to reveal the source of aggression.

He retched as he saw the man's inhumane eyes, unusually pale skin, and torn off flesh as his blood flooded the floor.

'Dr. Collins!' Eric threw the doctor away from himself and stepped back into the room. The doctor snarled sinisterly and walked toward Eric.

'I'm sorry I wasn't there to help you,' Eric sobbed, even though he knew he wasn't actually talking to Charles. 'I'm sorry.' He saw Alexis point his gun at Charles, waiting for confirmation. Eric closed his eyes and nodded. The very next moment he heard a gunshot.

Just as he chose to relax his body, he heard a yell. 'He's still alive!'

The wounds did not stop the doctor. The shots didn't seem to bother him. Blood forcefully gushed out of the bullet hole. The gun holders' hands started shivering in denial of what they had just witnessed.

'They usually fall on their knees after getting shot on their damned legs!' Alexis screamed.

'He's already dead! How many more times can we kill him?' Marcos yelled back.

'You're not making any sense!'

Besides the chaotic chatter, Charles was engrossed in his target—Eric. The two officers threw their guns and rushed toward Charles to hold him away from him. However, he had out powered them and managed to stretch his hands toward Eric. He grabbed his neck tightly and leaned toward him to tear his flesh with his filthy rotten teeth.

Eric was moved as he saw a strange furiousness in the doctor's eyes. He saw the desire to destroy, kill, and ruin lives. He knew nothing could have stopped the crime that was about to happen.

Just as he saw his death nearing, a bullet pierced straight through Charles's brain. A dark red liquid splattered all over Eric's face as he wrinkled his face tightly, stopping the infected blood from entering his body. He paused and let the incident sink in.

Charles fell dead on the floor, for real this time. Eric went out of breath and couldn't hear anything. He wanted to pause the world for a moment.

'Grace,' he whispered through his quivering lips as he saw her scared hands pointing the gun toward his direction. He let her walk toward him. 'How did you—'

'We met Roger; I know why this is happening—at least I think I do. I hope it is that but I don't hope it is. And I just shot his brains out and now he's dead?' Gracy vented tremulously as she started wiping off the doctor's blood from Eric's face. 'I almost lost you.'

'Grace, I think you saved my life.'

'We still have to evacuate the area. John Doe, remember?' Marcos wiped the fearful sweat off of his forehead while the body stared at him.

'Right, we'll start evacuating, take your time.' Alexis looked at the stunning couple.

'Are you hurt?' Gracy asked as she hoped for the answer to be a no.

'I'm OK—physically.'

'Oh, thank—'

'Just a scratch.'

Gracy was alarmed, she stared into his eyes and chose to withhold the information she had. She was well aware of what a scratch had done to Aaron.

'What?' Eric raised his eyebrows. Her reaction seemed pretty big for just a scratch.

'Nothing. Can I see it?'

He tilted his neck to the right and revealed a light red line. 'Just burns a little bit.' It was hardly visible.

'You'll be fine,' she tried to console herself. 'Let's just disinfect it.'

'Grace, it's just a scratch. Of course I'll be fine.'

Gracy ignored his words and found a first aid kit. She opened the treasure of medicines and tore a packet of rubbing alcohol. Eric tried studying her over protective actions as he watched her disinfect the wounds and seal them with a band-aid.

'Gracy, why do you look—'

'We have to warn the others!' She knew it was not the right time to reveal her hesitation.

They heard screams while running across the hallways. The officers started kicking the doors open, they were prepared for jump scares. While passing around the corner, Gracy bumped into a woman. She had turned into something else. Her body showed the same symptoms—blood-shot eyes and pale, torn skin. Her newly pressed white dress was covered in her own blood. The aggression in her eyes was the same as Charles's. While limping toward them, she growled atrociously.

They stepped back in horror. 'Ma'am, step back, or else I will have to shoot you.' Gracy pointed the gun at her, but the warning did not seem to bother the woman.

Eric looked at the limping body who walked toward them. She seemed anything but friendly.

Gracy held Eric's hand tightly and took an aim. She squeezed her eyes and asked, 'What do I do?'

'You're asking me?'

'No, the lady. Of course, I'm asking you!'

'How do you expect me to make this decision?' They argued over the infected woman's continuous groan.

'How do you expect me to shoot her?' Gracy's voice took a high-pitched tone as they watched the lady getting ready to pounce upon them. Gracy's both hands wrapped the gun firmly as she screamed loudly.

Two gunshots echoed in the corridor—both the bullets went straight through the woman's head. Her body slammed right on the floor as their motionless bodies stared at the blood gushing out.

'Gracy!' Poppy yelled as she ran toward them. 'Is it true?' Looking at the body, her question was answered. 'Looks like it is, I heard it from the boys.'

'Poppy, what're you doing here?' Gracy asked.

'I started to think you guys didn't need me anymore so 'Officer!'

'Eric, what's that on your neck?' Poppy asked in concern, unaware of how Gracy had been dodging the scratch situation.

'I got into an arm wrestle with an infected person. Just a scratch, I'm alright.'

'Gracy?' Poppy looked at her in worry. She decoded the message as Gracy slightly shook her head. 'We would've evacuated the area but we can't keep the doors wide open or these infected people will be out in the open and that's dangerous to the whole city. Everyone is scared, what do we do?'

'I don't know.' Gracy felt burdened. How could she answer all these questions with hers already piling up in her head? But the main reason she achieved the title of the youngest deputy superintendent was that she could work under pressure. She inhaled sharply and continued, 'You're right, don't leave the doors wide open. Call for backups, and I need you to ask the doctors and the nurses to stand near the gate and check for—'

'Symptoms. People who look pale, who look aggressive, quarantine them. Others are good to go,' Eric added as he recalled the common signs he noticed in both the infected.

The couple rushed toward the top floor to find it already evacuated. A short time span was found to process their surroundings. They stood there, reliving the moment of watching two doctors die.

'Hey!' Jacob and Zachery ran toward them.

'Floor's empty, huh?' Gracy sobbed.

'We—Eric? What's that?' Jacob interrupted his own sentence.

'A scratch.' Eric sighed. 'Had a tiff with one of the infected ones.' Eric started noticing the weird importance everyone had been giving to his barely visible wound.

'A scratch?!' Jacob yelled.

'Wow, what? Why is everyone—' Eric stopped and looked at Gracy.

Gracy looked back at him and speechless she stood there. The poor soul could not dodge his questions anymore.

Eric had to start preparing himself for the worst. 'Just tell me.'

Chapter 4: Uncontrollable

The human brain is interesting yet complicated. The brain stays alive for seven minutes after the heart stops beating rhythmically. A person has seven minutes to relive his entire life. Is it possible that a brain can hear and feel their loved ones for entire seven minutes? The brain is very delicate, a single parasite can ruin the whole central nervous system. For a moment, you see a bright light that gives you hope but within a second, the light is engulfed by a horrifying darkness and you lose everything you had, in just seven minutes. Pardon me, your loved ones lose everything they had. You'll be dead, you won't feel a thing, right?

A quarter of the city had already turned into a disaster. Murder and missing reports kept increasing and the cause was still a mystery. Many did not believe in what they heard. That is until they saw it happen right in front of their eyes. People were sent alert messages. A ridiculously loud warning siren followed by a message—*National Emergency Alert. Public movement and traffic shall be restricted from 10 pm tomorrow until further notice. Strict actions will be implemented against those who disobey.*

Rumor has it that there is a Zombie apocalypse. Of course, some people had only one thing to say to that, 'Zombies aren't real, stop watching silly movies.' However, people were unaware of what they were up against. The prank that the children used to play all the time, might be turning into reality. The virus did not stop spreading, it had become invincible. People fell sick and it only kept getting worse. The city was on a lock down and people were asked to lock all their doors and keep their hands sanitized.

It was two in the morning, and Linette's phone kept blowing up with calls and messages. Since the news got out that Aaron had come back home, all his colleagues' family members kept questioning Linette: What did your husband do? Where is he? How come he's back and my husband isn't?

She couldn't sleep with the ongoing questions. So, Linette being herself, got up and defended Aaron.

'How do you know that?' asked an angry voice from the other side of the phone. 'Listen! Aaron is also missing; I don't know where he is. Please try to understand!' Linette cried.

'OK, that is enough! Give me that!' Hunter snatched her phone and cut the call abruptly. 'I know you're a very calm person but you are not bound to answer these questions.'

'You know a little too much about me, don't you?'

'Linette, not right now,' he said politely. 'Kids are with Sophia upstairs, don't worry.' Hunter's hesitant hand held Linette's hand. She pressed a smile through her worried lips but couldn't muster her words.

'Injured body at Street 2. Reporting a dead body at Adams—' Heavy voices overlapped from the two-way radio.

Upon the realization of the situation happening around her, Linette withdrew her hand and asked, 'Could that be Aaron?'

Hunter was uncertain. He got up and strolled toward the window.

'Officer Gomez, come in.' But there was no response. 'Gomez!' he yelled at the radio hoping for some affirmation. 'Officer Yard, come in.' All the channels were unresponsive. Definitely, something was going on, everyone on duty was obligated to respond.

As he frowned and looked outside the window, his eyes caught a woman pouncing over a man as if she were trying to choke him. 'What the hell?' he whispered and rushed outside the house. He removed his gun and pointed it at them. 'Stop! Hands in the air, both of you!' He looked at the woman. 'State your name.'

'Carrie Taylor.' She smirked shamelessly.

'Officer! I'm Zander Taylor, her husband,' interrupted a drunken voice.

'What are you guys doing out here?'

'Sir, we're just—just playing around,' Zander stuttered as his weak hands started to relax.

'This city is under high alert, you both should be inside your house right now. Go home!' he yelled at them.

Zander wrapped Carrie's hand around his shoulders and walked toward their house as she chuckled drunkenly.

Hunter shook his head and slipped his gun back into his pocket as he went back inside.

'Zander and Carrie. They tend to display their emotions quite openly.' Linette barely smiled.

'Is that right?'

'They're nice people. You didn't have to point your gun at them.' Linette was scared to see a gun at her place.

Hunter's eyes wandered around the floor as he heard her go upstairs. He did not deny the fact that he did something wrong, but he chose to stay quiet as the environment was already screaming.

At Collin's Research Center.

'Eric, let's go home. This is not the right place to talk about it.' Gracy held his hand and rushed toward the car, passing through the chaotic crowd.

They started driving toward her house and with every kilometer, Eric's anxiety kept increasing. However, he chose not to question her. He knew Gracy would eventually tell him when it's time.

Finally, the muddy tires screeched as they had arrived at the point of mitigating Eric's suspense.

Linette heard them pull over and rushed downstairs. Her impatient soul opened the door before they could knock on it. 'Anything?' she asked from a distance, with hope.

'No.' Gracy and Eric walked toward the door.

Linette made way for them to enter and locked the door with her cold fingers.

'Gomez, Yard, Thomas, no one has been answering. Where are the officers? They were supposed to be in this perimeter by now,' Hunter complained.

Gracy sat down and seemed to be lost in her jumbled thoughts of miseries. It was the thought of Eric being in danger and most likely being *the* danger.

Eric sat down and wrapped his arms around her shoulder. 'Grace,' he whispered. He had waited long enough. His time to know what was happening was not far away.

She looked up and asked everyone to be seated, and so they did. She started off with Roger's story. Her voice had no emotions. Everything had been drained. 'And Aaron pushed Adrian off the ship.' She looked at Eric and watched him feel the wound through the band-aid. He realized that he could be infected with a deadly virus.

On completing the story, the room remained silent for a while.

'Are you saying that my husband is most likely to be hurting people right now or is dead?' Linette tried her best to hold her cry inside as she climbed downstairs.

'Am I going to be OK?' Eric looked at Gracy.

'We immediately disinfected your wound.' She looked back at him with anticipation.

The environment at Gracy's place was filled with fright. No one dared to utter a single word. Eric had Gracy sleeping on his shoulders as he caressed her soft brown hair between his fingers.

Linette sat on the floor as her legs pressed against her chest and her hands wrapped around it tightly. Her lips quivered with horror. Hunter sat down next to her, glazing at her beauty. Her face was messed up, yet her chaotic look was purely elegant. But he made sure she wasn't feeling uncomfortable with his admiration.

'Hunter, pass me a blanket, Gracy's shivering,' Eric whispered.

'I'll go upstairs to look for some, even Lin—Mrs. O'Malley is cold.' Hunter tiptoed up the staircase as he nodded his head.

On reaching Gracy's bedroom, he found Sophia sitting on the couch, uncomfortably. She blankly stared at the carpet and did not notice Hunter's presence. 'You're still up.' He removed two cream-colored blankets from an ancient-looking wardrobe.

'Oh, sir!' She bolted upright. 'I have a habit of staying up late.' Sophia rubbed her eyes.

Hunter smiled at her and exited the room. As soon as he was about to go downstairs, she stopped him. 'It can be false, right? The Roger story?'

'Take care of yourself, Sophia.' He went down to the living room. He himself was looking for answers.

'There,' Hunter whispered while handing over the blanket to Eric. He walked toward Linette and knelt down in front of her. Instead of wrapping it around her body, he kept the blanket beside her and walked away. He knew his limits.

A sleepy voice interrupted the silent environment. 'We should go to the center and check if everything is under control.'

'Hunter and I can go,' Eric replied.

Gracy disagreed as she got up and tied her hair into a bun. It gave her confidence; she was ready to face the outside world.

'Linette, you'll be OK?' Hunter asked in concern. She looked at him and nodded a yes, wondering why he cared.

Gracy couldn't seem to take her eyes off of Eric's scratch. Well, it wasn't getting worse, not yet at least.

They were off to the research center as Hunter took over the accelerator. He seemed the most stable, to take over the wheels, amongst the three.

Eric knew another pathologist who stayed nearby and decided to ring his number as he needed answers right away.

The clinical pathologist, Dr. Raghav Campbell, had a morgue built up at his house. He was always obsessed with the idea of a home morgue. The thought of his workplace being connected to his bedroom by a simple staircase made it convenient for him. He had a beautiful bungalow, the well-developed basement reserved only for the morgue.

With his experience of more than ten years of being a pathologist, he was quite famous in the city. Everyone looked forward to Raghav's views on what was happening. When Eric called him, he was already in for a biopsy. A body had come in around five hours ago and he hadn't stopped working on it since.

'You know, at first, I thought these are just cannibals going crazy. But as soon as this body was brought to me, I knew it was more than that. A normal human body would have never survived such injuries. He was shot four times, it seems. On his left leg, and right hand, the third one went straight through his heart but the police said that he was still alive. He died when he was shot in the head. Fourth's a charm now, I guess.' Raghav started spitting out all the information he had.

'Have you identified the virus yet?'

'Good question. I checked for Trichinella Spiralis, but no luck. No pork tapeworm, no Loa, no parasite.'

'Where was this body shot?'

'At Collin's center. I heard it's crazy out there.'

Eric sat up straight. 'Sir, I'll call you back again.' He cut the call immediately and asked Hunter to put a little more pressure on the accelerator.

At Collin's Research Center.

The situation went out of control. SWAT teams had surrounded the center. A smell of murder and puddles of thick red blood had taken over.

People seemed aggressive. They were screaming as gunshot noises increased. Some of them were just roaming around with scalpels like psycho serial killers, not caring who they slaughtered. Anyone near the center could fall into the hands of death.

Some of the insane and injured people managed to run away into the woods. It was safe to say that the streets of Annapolis weren't safe anymore.

Infected and healthy people, both had been running in the same chaotic crowd due to which the officers did not know whom to shoot and whom to spare. Their judgment wasn't good enough because they were certainly not trained for a day like this.

'They haven't called us yet; I think they have it under control.' Gracy's legs shook in nervousness.

'It could be two things,' Eric continued. 'Either they're completely in hand or—'

'Chaotic,' Hunter interrupted as he immediately jerked the car to a stop.

The center was in front of their eyes and it certainly wasn't the same as they last saw it. Everything was disrupted and had turned into a disaster.

From the car windows, they could see the shattered glass doors and windows of the building. The sound of the non-stop multi-barrel machine guns. Broken barriers. People running and going deranged. Kids sitting on the floor, lost and alone, crying and shrieking at the top of their voices. This scene was terrifying.

A five-year-old boy's cry attracted a man who carried a scalpel. He held it so tightly that it had cut through his palm—that didn't bother him. He stood beside the boy as the scared little voice yelled, 'Daddy!' No one knew what was going to happen next—will the man drop the scalpel seeing his child? Or will he manslaughter his own progeny?

The latter. The man wiped off his tears and spoke to the boy. 'I am sorry Jordan, daddy is very sorry.' He surely did not seem sorry. The very next moment, he lifted his arm, curling his fingers around the scalpel tightly, in an intention to give a firm stab. Hunter immediately opened the car door and shot a bullet through his brain. This scene was excruciating to watch—for the officers and for the five-year-old boy. His cry did not stop.

'How could a father try to?' Gracy's voice was barely audible.

'No, he tried repulsing. That wasn't him. Gracy, he was infected.' Eric observed the pale-yellow skin.

They stepped out of the car as their eyes caught Jacob and Poppy taking cover behind a black jeep. They ran toward them.

'What happened here?' Gracy yelled through her gritted teeth in a hushed voice. Poppy looked down in disappointment and gave Gracy a straight answer. 'The SWAT opened only one of the gates and barricaded every other. They let the uninfected ones out through those gates. Now, the ones who behaved differently and seemed infected, they were quarantined behind gate five. People started getting frustrated and—'

'And I decided to open up another gate,' Jacob added. 'Gracy, people were trapped inside with those infected ones, you would've—anyway, I got the permission of opening gate two but these systems were so confusing and you know I'm too proud to ask for help so I tried to figure it out all by myself and opened all the gates, including gate five. People ran outside and broke the crowd control barriers.'

Gracy looked at Jacob through her furious eyes. 'You have been ignorant since day one and I did not utter a word about it thinking you will get better. But today you were careless!' Gracy slammed her hand on the ground.

The human brain is unpredictable, it acts out whenever it wants to, without a warning.

Eric was going to add to Gracy's rage but he calmed himself down because a slight arrogant gesture would worry everyone, especially Gracy. He had locked his words inside a box and thrown it far away from his vocal box.

Jacob slowly lowered his eyes in embarrassment. He knew Poppy would get mad at him for throwing himself under the bus. The story was true but the person who actually deserved to be yelled at—was Poppy. Gracy's words mean a lot to her, he thought. It's better if I take the blame. I don't care as much.

'Since you've created this nuisance, might as well give a good idea how to control it.' Gracy looked at the condition of the center and nodded.

Getting no idea from anyone, Gracy scoffed and sat there cluelessly as she leaned on the car. After a few silent minutes, Gracy pushed herself forward. 'Outside the center—not safe anymore. I guess the inside is. Take every sane person inside and isolate them. Once everyone is inside, I need a full lock down.'

'What about those who are trying to hurt people?' Jacob asked.

Gracy looked at him and sighed in frustration. 'Warn them I guess.'

'Shoot them.' Eric looked at Gracy's gun and felt relieved, he smiled. He did not know where the feeling emerged from but it was there and it was evident.

Gracy lifted her eyes up to Eric's and felt strange energy around him.

'Eric?'

'What?' He pretended as if his words were not wrong.

'We have to go warn the leader.'

They rushed toward the SWAT who carried heavy-armed weapons, protecting themselves in a bunch of armored layers. It was easy to spot the leader—asserting personality, an invisible scare on the face, a lack of hesitation, and a clear voice.

'Inspector Valerie Clinton.' Gracy walked toward her.

'Officer Brown, aren't you?'

'Yes, ma'am.'

'I see the deputy superintendent is out here, where must be the main man?'

'I fear he's out of the country.'

'Refreshing!'

There was a moment of awkward silence in the midst of the madness. It was never intimidating for Gracy to face a power that held a superior post. She always freezes in front of them, thinking why people get intimidated so easily.

'If I may, I suggest we put everyone back inside and quarantine them.' She did not expect any negative responses.

'Good thinking.' Without questioning Gracy's idea, Inspector Clinton commanded her team to follow Gracy's orders.

Before they even knew it, everyone was inside and the open field near the center was empty and tranquil.

However, there were more than fifty bodies lying dead on the ground. Imagine seeing all that in one view—it made people puke their lungs out, it made them cry, it made them mentally sick.

'What is happening?' Gracy stared at an infant's body covered with blood.

Eric looked at her sympathetically. He did not have answers to her questions, no one did. The virus had probably made its way into every healthy soul. The infected ones were still out there and nothing was going to stop them from spreading this mayhem.

Chapter 5: Farewell, My Friend

The human brain is stubborn. It's tough to feed sense into the brain. Sometimes, it blurs out everything and makes you do something you should not—it plays you. Most of the time, the brain is just curious. It knows not to push the button, but it still does. It would press it a million times. It will make you do things that you are restricted to do. You know it is wrong but your brain does not accept it until you do it. Something similar happened during this epidemic. Some people stayed home, whereas the others were so intrigued with what was happening around them that it made them go out and "explore." Even after being completely aware of the situation, they did not want to believe it until they saw it happening right in front of them. Who wouldn't be tempted to see a man eat a man?

Eric had colleagues that were fond of taking up challenges. Maverick Miller, one of the craziest investigators and Eric's ride-or-die bitch. Along with his beautiful wife, Maverick had settled in New York—their dream place. Unfortunately, right after two years of their marriage, she died due to Cystic Fibrosis. He had gone into complete denial and had to get out of it to get his life together. A random newspaper showed him a path—a new job in Annapolis. He couldn't stay in New York; it would only remind him of his beloved wife.

He took the opportunity and moved to Annapolis, where he continued his profession as an investigator.

He got into Eric's team and had been investigating cases with them for two years. Eric was always fond of his work. There was this crazy passion in Maverick—he would refuse to blink even once until he was satisfied with his investigation. He was a perfectionist.

At Collin's Research Center.

A sense of calmness in the air finally took over, but not for long.

'Poppy, you're in charge. Hunter, Eric, and I are going back to my house. Take these bodies to the center' Gracy's voice went downhill. 'I am sure these people have families, let them know where they are. Do not let the media capture this—it's highly sensitive and I don't trust any cameras around this center.' They walked toward her car.

'Poppy! That five-year-old kid—Jordan, was it? Call the social services for him, OK?' Hunter looked at her and made her know that the child was their top priority. Poppy responded to that with a firm yes and went back inside.

The trio got into the car and off they went.

On the way, Eric received a call from Maverick.

'Eric, my boy! Where are you?' Maverick's voice took an exciting road.

Eric yawned. 'I've been busy at the Collins' Center. Uh, Charles—'

'Well, I'm with Clover, Hendricks, and Ayden, near Dr. Raghav's. There are two dead bodies here and to be honest, it's quite disturbing but also very cool, you've got to see this!'

Eric bolted upright and yelled, 'No, leave that area immediately! It's not safe out there, take a look at the news for god's sake!'

'I don't care what the news says.' Was it not mentioned how crazy Maverick Miller was? 'We need answers to this. Besides, how deadly can it be? Hm, quite a contradiction cause I'm literally looking at two messed up bodies.' His voice sounded disgusted.

'Maverick, don't go near them. I've seen—'

'I am not leaving, be there or be square! See ya!' Maverick hung up the phone.

Eric huffed. 'Stupid.' He asked Hunter to pull over. Gracy was already paranoid, leaving her alone with her deadly thoughts was probably not a good idea. However, Eric had to save his friends from the bodies that might come to life soon.

Gracy handed her gun over to him. 'Use it wisely.' As he got out of the car, he turned around and smiled at Gracy to lighten up her mood. It worked.

He walked a little further in search of his team and noticed a few people arm wrestling. He let out a frustrated sigh as he sprinted toward him. Pulling the bolt of the Beretta M9, he pointed the gun at the scene and concentrated on his aim. He knew he had to pull the trigger. One man, carrying the same symptoms as those who were infected, wrestled Maverick and had him down on the ground. The other man choked Clover as Ayden and Hendricks tried pulling him away from her. The men growled as blood splattered, painting their faces with red stains.

'Stand back!' Eric yelled.

Hendricks and Ayden took his orders post-haste and witnessed him pull the trigger twice. His shots perfectly pierced through both the brains and the infected men were on the ground. Surprisingly, he didn't mind the bloodshed.

'Did I not warn you about this?' Eric stomped toward Maverick and kicked his lying body.

'They were dead! We checked their pulse!' Maverick yelled back at him, trying to pick himself up.

'They come alive!'

'What do you mean they come alive?'

'I don't know!' They started yelling at each other while others stared at the still bodies. The two of them did not stop bickering. However, at a point, Eric had to stop to make sure no one got hurt. It was uncommon to go through a cat fight and not get a single scratch, but these were a bunch of lucky investigators. None of them had a single wound to panic upon.

'What are these?' Ayden shivered. 'And why are they so yellow?'

'What is happening?' Hendricks added to the list of doubts.

'It's a long story. All I can say is that there is a virus outbreak and the symptom is violence. Well, apparently if their blood meets your blood you turn into one of them.' Eric lowered his voice, trying not to sound strange.

'Like zombies?!' Ayden exclaimed.

'Mother of God, I was hoping none of you would mention that silly term, who even are you?' Eric looked at Ayden, trying to recall if he had seen him before.

'I'm Ayden Stone. New here.'

'You're not new to this world, are you? Don't use that term again.'

'Very accurate with the explanation, huh? We can *see* they're violent, Eric.' Maverick went up to him. 'What's the back story?'

Eric was hesitant. Repeating a story that would remind him of his scratch did not seem ethical to his soul. But would he let others stay in the dark only to spare his own emotions?

'I'll tell you at Dr. Campbell's.'

'I would rather get infected and isolate myself,' Clover whispered. She wasn't quite fond of that man. Maybe because he was never fond of her either. It just worked for them—not liking each other's company.

'I spoke to him a few hours ago. He's working on a body. Maybe my story would help his research and your intrigued brains would finally be satisfied being a part of some investigation.'

'How are we supposed to get there?' Ayden asked, seeing no transport at the farthest.

'Good question.' Eric stared at him for a while as Ayden started realizing that they weren't far away from Raghav's home morgue. 'It's right there, Stone.' He pointed to a house, just a block away.

Ayden felt stupid but he managed to smile away throughout their small walk. The villa was different from the others. You would think it was dark as a monster house because it had dead bodies living inside of it. Not really.

The villa was a beauty, it was the definition of magnificent. She stood there with pleasing colors of cream white and light turquoise. Her garden bloomed like spring was a never-ending season. She did not carry any flaws with her, only boldness and pride.

'This is the morgue?' Ayden's jaw dropped.

'Impressive, huh?' Eric opened the gate and stepped into the lawn as if entering his own. 'The residing dead bodies they're disturbing for the neighbors, especially their kids. The colors Raghav used for his house—happy and easy to look at. The existence of this place is no longer an issue.'

'And that's who Dr. Raghav Campbell is.' Maverick smiled proudly.

'Quite impressive,' Ayden admired the compassion.

Eric did not resist knocking on the door incessantly. A grumpy 50-year-old man opened the door. Due to a lack of luminosity, Ayden failed to see the mastermind behind the idea of a beguiling home morgue. Beguiling and morgue in the same sentence? That's not very common.

'Why at this hour?' asked a croaky voice from the other side of the door.

'Why?' Maverick mocked. 'Why can't you just appreciate our presence for once?'

'Huh.' Dr. Campbell scoffed as he made way for them to enter. 'Like that's ever going to happen.' He switched on the lights as they pierced through everyone's squinting eyes. The light shone upon the spacious hall with vinyl walls.

The house was beautifully maintained, with marble flooring and everything was kept neatly where it belonged. It was a house of a disciplined family. There was a strong, yet calm essence. Rose water mixed with that lavender came from the majestic red curtain. No one could ever tell that it was also a morgue. The elegant chandeliers that hung from the ceiling, twelve feet above, reflected how affluent Raghav Campbell was.

Raghav knew he had to take them to his morgue, he knew he was looking at curious minds. He led them to his morgue through a compact stairwell that was placed in the corner of the house. As they went one floor under, the environment had completely changed. Reaching the last step of the staircase, five meters away, stood a heavy steel slab. As Raghav likes to call it—the doorway to hell.

Ayden's horrified face was all over the place, Raghav couldn't ignore it. 'Just because this door looks like a barrier between life and death doesn't mean it really is one. Secured doors like this keep my children from entering and traumatizing themselves.' He looked at Ayden whilst pressing the six-digit combination code to unlock the heavy steel. He had done this countless times, he didn't even have to look at the numbers – *6 1 0 9 1 5* – his fingers managed to find the buttons on their own.

As they walked through the gateway, each one got their own hazmat suits and scrubs. 'Could be a deadly virus.' Raghav's muffled voice spoke through his mask. The ground floor was quite interesting—seemed different from the upstairs, of course. The walls were painted in dark gray and the sweet essence was no longer existent. There were four doors—the first two opposites were the morgue and the room where all the unclaimed bodies were kept. The one on the far right was another steel slab, a back entrance for the dead bodies to enter. The fourth door was a mystery.

Raghav noticed Ayden peeping inside one of the rooms. 'All the dead bodies are laid in there, not really a pleasant watch. I wouldn't do whatever you're doing right now.'

'What? Yes! Of course, sir I wasn't going to—'

'This way, gentlemen.'

'And a lady,' Clover whispered.

They entered the room on the near right, where an obnoxious odor struck their nose, which was next to unbearable. The room had blood splattered all over the floor—it surely did not seem welcoming. It was rather a busy place, where papers with bloody hand prints were scattered on the study table, an indecent amount of test tubes carrying thick red blood, and a soft board that had newspapers and research printouts pinned against it.

This only reminded Eric of what he had seen in the Research Center. He froze as his legs refused to enter the room. He relived the terrible moment of being strangled by his own mentor. Seeing him lost in deep thoughts, Maverick shook him out of it and brought him into reality. 'What's been bothering you lately?' he asked and watched Eric's eyes flicker. Before Eric could reply to that, both the men got distracted by the open dead body, lying on the table.

The body was wrinkled and showed only one color yellow. Dr. Campbell had cut him open from wherever he could. It was safe to say that he had done some serious digging on this case.

'Before you go near this body, let me enlighten you with a few things I happened to come across.' Raghav's voice took a proud tone. 'This John Doe was brought to me four hours ago from the research center. The only thing we know about him is literally nothing. He was shot four times—once on his leg, his hand, and a third time through his heart. It seems he was still alive. But when a bullet went through his head he fell right to the ground. His body has been rotting since—'

'Can I see his face?' Eric recognized the body. His brain could picture it as someone he knew, but it was a blur. Was it Charles? Was it someone he had bumped into the previous day? Was it one of Gracy's friends? He had to obliterate this curiosity.

'I am not done with my explanation yet.' Raghav's polite voice sounded impatient.

'I think I can identify him.'

'Alright, everyone can come to take a closer look.' He smothered his emotions of being interrupted.

A sudden flashback hit Eric's memory when he saw a plastic bag containing John Doe's clothes. He had seen the worn-out blue shirt before in the midst of chaos—he was chasing those clothes.

The man's face was covered with a white cloth, soaked with patches of his own blood. Eric reached out to the cloth and slowly lifted it from the top corner. All eyes, except for Raghav's, were focused on the body's face reveal, waiting to see the man who took a bullet to his heart and still did not give up on his life. And finally, the cloth was off his identity was out there.

The fabric fell from Eric's partially pinched fingers as he stepped back. 'He's not John Doe.' He took a while before unraveling the name. 'His name is Aaron

O'Malley and his wife is waiting for him to return.' His brain played on memories of Linette's optimistic thoughts about her healthy, alive husband.

'I would advise you to leave if you know this man.' Raghav sighed.

'No,' he whispered. 'I have to take him to his wife.'

'In the middle of my research?' Raghav raised his voice in frustration.

Eric was silent.

'His body is rotting' Raghav's polite voice came back. 'Usually, after death, it takes a day or two for the body to rot. And normally, the body temperature would fall by one point five degrees Fahrenheit, every hour, until the blood reaches room temperature. But this body's temperature is rising and I can't seem to stop it by any cooling method. Hell, I got so frustrated I kept a slab of ice on him—worked a little. Now, mostly the skin would gradually fall off but his skin and bones are melting. Forget rare, this isn't supposed to happen at all. There's only one possible reason for this reaction—the aggressive virus inside him. I believe it'll keep behaving this way until it dies out or maybe find a healthier host to control. I ran many tests; this virus is completely unknown. It could be an undiscovered ancient virus. We don't know how it got into John Doe's body.'

'His name is Aaron,' Eric stated.

Raghav looked at him, still controlling his furiousness, and corrected himself. 'Aaron's body.'

Maverick looked at Raghav and asked, 'How did this man take a bullet through his heart and still did not end up dead?'

A loud bang interrupted their conversation. To their shock, they watched Eric hyperventilate as he stood near the knocked-over tools. The disturbed look on his face was loud and clear.

'Man, what is up with you?' Hendricks stressed his words.

'Give him some space, he just witnessed his friend's body.' Maverick always had Eric's back.

Raghav frowned and commanded, 'I know you Eric, you couldn't have taken this lightly. Maverick, take him and leave.'

Without uttering another word, Maverick grabbed Eric's arms and walked out of the house. Eric put in no effort during the walk, he was dragged by his friend.

'Gracy's house?' Maverick asked as they stepped out in the open.

'Yeah,' replied Eric in a toneless voice.

Her house was close enough, they walked along the footpath with their eyes wide open. 'Care to fill in about that breakdown?' Maverick broke the silence.

Telling Maverick about the scratch would have been a bad decision. Eric looked at him and sighed. 'Never imagined Aaron lying on that table. His cold or warm—whatever, yellow body stared at me, Mave. It's not gonna be easy informing his wife about this.'

At Gracy's place.

She impatiently waited before the noise of the trilling line, trying to reach Eric's phone. Her restive legs tapped against the ground as she gazed outside the window, hoping to get a quick sight of Eric walking toward her.

'He'll be back.' She heard a silvery voice.

'Morning, Linette.' Gracy watched her come downstairs.

'You know, I was just thinking about all the things I'm going to yell to Aaron when he comes back home.' She chuckled. 'He's in so much trouble.'

Gracy's smile wore off as she looked away. 'I hope he's out there.'

'Eric?'

'Aaron.'

'There you go women, stay hydrated.' Hunter put down two glasses of fresh orange juice. 'Sophia's asleep?'

Linette quietly nodded to his question, as she slowly swallowed down the liquid. 'Then that's two glasses of orange for me!' Hunter exclaimed.

'Hunter, thank you for this.' Gracy chugged it down.

'Yeah, thank you Hunter.' Linette smiled as she carefully placed the half-empty glass on the table. Hunter smiled back at her, settling on the arm chair, opposite them.

'I just squeezed out some oranges, no big deal,' Hunter murmured.

'You're too humble. Why don't you ever think about getting married?' Gracy squinted her eyes at him.

Hunter pulled himself forward and chuckled nervously. His serious emotions took over as he played with the circumference of the glass. 'There was this one woman I really loved, she left me for another man.'

'She's not the last female in this world, you know? I've never seen you mess around as the others do.' Gracy was intrigued.

'I got busy with work.'

'You can take a long vacation.'

'Like you'd allow that.'

'Not a chance.' Gracy smiled weakly as Linette was fidgeted with her fingers.

Again, a quieter environment took over. It broke again when two men were heard on the street outside the house.

'Uh, did she say yes?' Maverick's voice was clear to them.

The men were heading back home. Eric had dispelled Gracy's anxiety. She rushed to open the door.

Eric looked at Maverick with a playful smirk. 'Duh.'

'Hey Mave, it's been long!' Gracy exclaimed as the men walked inside the house.

'It has, hasn't it? Congrats on the ring!' Maverick shook his hand.

Everyone settled down in the living room, except for Linette—who went to fetch some water for the boys.

'Gracy, I see you make this man very happy. He was so upset when he saw that body,' said Maverick as he watched Eric caress Gracy's hair.

'What body?' Gracy moved away from him.

Eric threw a frustrated look at Maverick and sighed. 'We went to Dr. Campbell's place and he was performing an autopsy on a body. It was Aaron's, we found Aaron—'

'You found Aaron?' Linette's naive face looked at them expectantly as everyone looked down. No one was ready to break the news to her.

'Wha—well, where is he?' Her foolish smile looked at them.

'You're his wife?' Maverick gulped.

'I'm his wife, yes! Where is he?' She started getting impatient.

'Mrs. O'Malley, we found your husband's body.'

'What do you—what are you saying?' Linette's smile wore off.

'Aaron is dead.' Eric pressed his lips.

'No,' Linette whispered. 'What are you saying?' Her voice got louder, fighting for breath. 'That can't be true!' she yelled and blubbered. Her eyes had already turned red. Her nose turned cold blue. She couldn't hear or feel herself breathe. She didn't even know if she was breathing. Voices got muffled around her and everything went numb. She didn't know where she was, her heartbeat was the only thing she felt. She blankly stared at the carpet through her blurry, teary vision as it started getting pitch black.

Hunter sat beside Linette and shushed her. She cried into his arms as his light brown shirt turned dark with her sorrowful tears. While everyone looked away,

Gracy's vision was stuck on Eric's wound as she imagined herself in Linette's position.

'Grace Mave can I speak to you both in private?' Eric took them to the kitchen.

'I snapped.' There was fear in his voice.

'No, I'm sure it was because of the body you saw.' Of course, Gracy wanted to keep her thoughts positive at all times.

'I'm lost.' Maverick frowned.

'I guess I have the virus. Dr. Charles had turned into one of those and tried strangling me. Clearly, I got away with that but he pierced his nails in my neck and I think I have the virus.'

'You don't! Mave, I sanitized his wound right after!' Gracy panicked as she watched Maverick hold his forehead with absolutely no expression on his face.

'Nothing will happen to you.' Maverick stated in denial.

'Yeah, right.' Eric scoffed and walked away.

Gracy nodded her head and looked at Maverick. 'He's just paranoid.' They consoled themselves.

As they all went back to the hall, they found Linette's mood to be quieter. She sobbed in abrupt breathing intervals, still burying herself in Hunter's arms.

'Can I see him?' asked Linette.

'Not yet,' Eric whispered.

Her cry had woken up the kids. 'Mommy?' Nathan rubbed his eyes and yawned innocently.

'Nate! Go upstairs and play! No school today.' Gracy faked a smile and watched him run upstairs in joy. She relaxed her face and sighed.

Gracy's phone caught a signal and her phone suddenly started blowing up. 'Seriously?' She unlocked her phone and found a new number messaging her. Thirteen messages from an unknown number? She thought. On opening the chat, she clenched her eyes and looked away. They were more images of people's rotting bodies—images of dead children's torn faces, eaten-off skin, and fresh blood oozing out. *'Look at what you nincompoops have done,'* said the messages, in between the image spam.

'What's this?' Gracy whispered to herself. She scrolled down to the latest message where it said, *'This is just the beginning.'*

Chapter 6: Grief

The human brain is playful. When someone dies, it makes you think about that person more than ever. It will constantly make you hear and see those people who have recently died in the least expected way. You would not be able to stop thinking about the events leading up to their death. This happens because sometimes the brain is trying to process death and acknowledge the finality of it.

Linette sat on the sofa, drowned in thoughts. What would have happened if she had paid more attention to him? Could she have saved him from death? She felt nauseous but did not have the energy to throw up. Her eyes couldn't focus on any object, not even on her kids—who were trying to shake her, get her back into her senses. All she could hear was their restless questions about their father and where he was. How could she reply to that? She shifted uncomfortably and looked at Gracy.

She looked back at her, helpless. 'Kids maybe you should—'

'I think I have the right to know where my father is!' Samantha yelled.

'He's dead!' Not regretting the hurtful words coming out of her mouth, Linette looked straight into Samantha's eyes.

Samantha pressed her lips and froze. She slowly nodded her head in disagreement, trying to let the event sink in. She allowed tears to break free as her arms looked for a comforting hug.

'I'm taking my children back to my place.' Linette stood up and grabbed Nathan's hand and walked outside the door. No one stopped her.

Samantha looked at Eric. They went along well—Eric always wanted a little sister and Samantha, for a change, wanted an elder brother. She only hoped she heard her mother wrong. 'Is that true or is my mother going mad as a hatter?' On getting silence as a confirmation, she sobbed and ran toward her house.

Eric exhaled through his mouth and banged the wall with his closed fist, as Gracy winced at his hostility. She watched him stomp up the stairs, without apologizing for his behavior.

'Uh, make sure we have officers looking after every street,' she whispered to Hunter and walked away.

There are five stages of grief. Denial, anger, bargaining, depression, and acceptance. People forget to mention another stage that follows no one ever likes to talk about it. Why? The attitude it carries is just insensitive! Moving on with someone else. Sometimes, it so happens that another person is able to take the place of the one who has died. It is certainly not easy to get over someone you have been with for years; however, it is not impossible for that to happen either how real, how insensitive.

Denial, anger, bargaining. Stages that Linette experienced simultaneously. She did not want to accept Aaron's death; she was furious at every event—she yelled at a chair for being slightly misplaced. But she also was preparing herself for the worst acceptance. Who knew accepting someone's death could be worse than death itself.

Life had become meaningless to her, she felt nothing but suffering. And once again, her place was soundless.

At Gracy's place.

'I'm heading to the library. Wait for my call—I know I'll get something today,' Maverick sounded cocky. Usually, when he is confident, everything falls in place for him. And every time it does, he receives an eye roll from Eric. "Cheeky" Maverick is something Eric would like to eliminate from his life permanently.

'Right, go safe.' Eric watched him parade down the street. And there it was—the ultimate eye roll.

Meanwhile, Hunter did not seem comfortable leaving Linette alone at her house with her traumatized brain. He found himself useless at Gracy's house. 'Can I go check on Mrs. O'Malley?'

'That'll be great.' Gracy politely let out her voice and saw him rush outside. 'Isn't Sophia still upstairs?' she asked in the empty hallway.

'Ma'am!' a voice shrieked from the middle staircase.

'Ah! You are still at my place.'

'Oh, I'm sorry, I can leave.'

'Wha—no! I'm glad you're here. I'm sending you a phone number. I need this phone's user in front of me by tomorrow.'

'I've seen this number somewhere.' Sophia harshly rubbed her eyes and stared into the screen. 'Right! The person who sent us those images in the first place!'

'The ones who were declared as a hoax? Are you sure?'

'I have a photographic memory and—'

'Beautiful. Send it to Poppy, I need to see this person who has the audacity to mess with a deputy superintendent.'

'Right away.'

Gracy looked at her phone and decided to take the conversation to the next step. 'I'm assuming there's a reason why you're sliding into my messages.' She sent it without hesitation.

In less than a minute, she got a reply. This mysterious person behind the screen seemed to have a lot of time in hand. 'No. I just want you people to know that going to Fenjiyawa was a big mistake. Enjoy the chaos.'

'Going to Fenji—' She felt as if she was being watched by someone. She locked her phone and kept it in her tight back pocket. On turning around, she found Eric's irritated frown staring at her. 'Eric?' She fidgeted with her hair.

'Where is it, Gracy?' he asked, raucously.

'Where is what?'

'The ring I gave you.'

'I have it!' She swayed her left hand, showing the shining ruby on her finger, at Eric.

'Give it back!' he yelled. Words came out of his mouth without permission. 'You don't deserve it, just like the title you have at the police station!'

Gracy swallowed hard and took a few steps back. His words had stabbed her motivation a hundred times, shattering her into tiny pieces. She had never seen this side of him, mainly because he never had a side that was this relentless.

A few minutes into the dreadful furiousness, she watched him go through a jerk of realization—a flicker in his eyes. He looked at Gracy's frightened face and muttered, 'What am I doing here?'

'You snapped at me,' she whispered and frowned as if she was looking at a newly evolved Eric. It was the virus acting up when she realized that her inner self broke down even more.

On the other hand, Eric tried his best to recall the event but couldn't seem to remember any part of it. He looked back at Gracy. 'I am so sorry, I don't remember anything, it wasn't me.' He loathed the fact that he had raised his voice in front of his innocent caring woman.

Gracy went closer to wrap him in her scarred arms. However, they got even more shivery when she felt his body temperature rising up. 'Are you feeling OK?'

He started complaining about feeling nauseous as his body turned pale yellow. Gracy wasn't ready to give up on him. The thoughts of him turning into one of those people ripped her heart apart. However, she let go of the fatalistic thoughts and replaced them with positive ones—a true sanguine. She took him upstairs and gave him a few medicines to help his boiling temperature.

On retrieving downstairs, she found Sophia minding her own business. 'I'm sorry you had to see that.'

'Don't worry about that. I barely heard anything.'

'I doubt that.'

'Uh, Poppy asked me to tell you that everything is under control at the center.'

'That's how I like it.' Gracy nodded and saw a ray of hope.

At Linette's place.

Hunter was at Linette's doorstep, trying to rehearse his lines before going in. 'Mrs. O'Malley! Nice house—no, that's dumb.' His eyes were drawn to an already opened door. 'Wait, what the hell?' He immediately reached out for his gun and slightly kicked the door open, with the gun against his chest. As he walked inside steadily, Linette appeared in front of him with a knife in her hand, with an intention to stab the invader.

'Mrs. O'Malley!' Hunter pulled away from his gun, pointing it away from Linette.

'Hunter? You gave me a fright!' Linette rested her hand and let out a sigh of relief.

'My apologies I didn't mean to startle you. The door was open so—'

'This door?' She pointed out to the half-open, creaking wood.

'Which other door could I be possibly talking—'

'Samantha! Nathan!' she yelled out loud, clearly aware of the fact that she had locked the door thoroughly.

'Isn't Nathan with you?' Samantha sobbed, still not over her father's death.

Linette looked at Hunter as they both ran outside in search of the little boy. Everything unfortunate took place. Linette could not believe that the universe was acting up against her, again.

At Gracy's place.

Eric tried putting himself to sleep. His eyes started to burn as he closed his eyes; however, he knew he needed to rest them and so he shut his eyes as tightly as he could. As he got used to the burning sensation, a strange feeling on his right arm woke him up. His blurry eyes tried searching for the source of the interference. To his shock, he noticed his nerves popping out as the area on the skin swelled up. He bolted upright and rubbed the area to settle it down. Ten seconds into his panic, the swelling had disappeared.

'I'm hallucinating.' He consoled himself and went back to sleep.

A few minutes later, when Eric got to shut his brain down peacefully, his phone desperately vibrated. He growled uncomfortably and rolled to the other side of the bed to receive the call. He inhaled sharply. 'Yes, Mave?'

'Ah, you were sleeping.' Maverick smacked his lips and continued. 'Well now that you're awake, let me educate you with something my beautiful brain just discovered.'

'Don't you mean your cocky brain?'

'You're just envious.'

'You got me.'

'This virus, there's no mention of it in any modern research books—'

'Great discovery.'

'But! Since I'm a genius man, I snuck into the old, abandoned archived library and got myself the most ancient book ever. But guess what? I got nothing!'

'Does this story have a productive ending?'

'Wait for it, lad. That's when it clicked in my mind. My father used to read me a book, the legend of Nicodemus the tenth where Nicodemus was a brave ruler and Aristarchus was just an A-hole.'

'Great, a fantasy.'

'Eric, shut up and listen. I managed to find it and underneath that amazing pile of dust, there it was, the symptoms we've been seeing all around us. This virus was created by Aristarchus with pure resentment because apparently our friend Nico here had this amazing life and of course, the throne. Guess where it all happened.'

'Fenjiyawa?'

'Fenjiyawa.'

'Maverick, don't ever lose that cocky brain of yours.' Eric disconnected the call and rushed down the stairs. This lead was an important piece of the puzzle. On reaching downstairs, he found Gracy and Sophia staring into the phone as if they had found an even bigger lead. 'What is it?'

Gracy was startled. She opened her mouth, but words couldn't seem to come out of it. So, she nodded and handed her phone over to him.

'See for yourself.' She let out a frustrated sigh, still waiting for her team to fish this person out of the mystifying river. She watched Eric's face get colorless as he kept scrolling.

'How dare he—' Before he could cuss more, a new message had arrived. He read out loud, 'Nathan is a sweetheart.'

On the streets.

Linette and Hunter cried Nathan's name out loud. A few minutes into the yelling, they heard a loud cry from a distance. Hunter managed to run toward the source of the shrieking voice. To his shock, he found Nathan sitting on the road, with absolutely no presence of another soul.

Linette heaved her son with her cold, shivering hands. She took the traumatized child back inside the shelter and quietened him. 'Mommy's right here, Nate.'

Hunter wandered around the neighborhood but couldn't find anyone. The sun was shining aggressively on the road, there was absolutely no way for a child to walk on it for at least more than six meters, without getting their sensitive feet burnt. However, the streets were silent. There were no signs of a human presence.

Linette's place was as dull as those gray clouds in mid-monsoon. There were no concerns left in her for anyone but her family. She kept disappearing with time, and she was aware of it. 'Thanks for stopping by. If it weren't for you, I would've lost Nathan. You can leave now,' she said while watching Nathan run upstairs to his worried sister.

'No, let me stay,' he pleaded.

Linette inclined her face toward Hunter and questioned, 'Why are you doing this?'

'I just want to make sure that your family is alright.'

'I appreciate your concerns but you have to leave.'

'Someone managed to break into your house and took Nathan! There should be a sane, vigilant adult in this house!'

'I can't have you around me just please.' Tears rolled down her cheeks, uncontrollably.

'You're not bringing up the past now, are you?' On getting no reply, Hunter shook his head and showed himself out of her house. He sat on her doorstep, his head facing downward to save itself from the sharp glare of the sun, and started drowning in a sweet memory lane that took a different path, a major throwback.

Linette McCarthy and Hunter Callahan. This acquaintance started the moment they were born. Their families were close and like any other cliché parents, dreamed of their children being together someday—at least confidants, if not more.

As they hit eighteen, their families planned a trip, without the new adults. Things fell apart when news about a bridge collapse was heard. None of their parents were able to survive the fall. Since then, they grew up supporting each other and eventually started dating.

They both joined the same university, pursuing to be a cop. A lot of weeks passed by, and studies and hard work created a lot of distance between them. Mainly because Hunter was more than determined toward having a well-secured future for them. Whereas Linette was uncomfortable with being distant, it threw her off her game.

On realizing this, they decided to step back for a while till she could figure out her life as Hunter moved into an even bigger apartment. He was never going to isolate her forever, he waited for the right time to pop the question.

On the other hand, Linette felt estranged, she had no idea about the bigger picture and forced herself to move on. It didn't take her time. A month later, she found someone that made her feel equally special and important—Aaron O'Malley. She was confused about what to call him when he was not around.

Love or a rebound? Soon, she succeeded in convincing herself that it was love, but she had a little secret along with it.

Weeks into their relationship, Hunter had called her over to catch up for the old time's sake. The innocent reunion wasn't friendly anymore. They had their moment and ended up in bed, beside each other, panting as they recall their amazing time. While watching Hunter's satisfied face, she was drowning in guilt as he had no clue about her relations with Aaron.

She kept her so-called relations with both the men till she could figure a way out of this triangle. After putting a lot of thought into it and when unexpected news arrived, she decided to end her future with Hunter. Why? She carried Aaron's progeny.

'I don't get it. Even after knowing that I cheated on you, you're ready to parent this child with me?' Young Linette, in her 20s, asked Aaron.

'It's gonna hurt a lil bit but I'm ready to overlook all that and start a new life with you. Will you marry me, Linette?' Aaron got on his knees as he watched her say yes.

The naive lady didn't even have the time to update Hunter about her life. On getting a call from him, while she was peacefully meditating, she realized she had left someone hanging. How am I so irresponsible? She thought to herself. What am I gonna tell him?

On the other hand, Hunter had been planning something big for them. His poor, hope-filled soul was ready to start a new life with her. Little did he know, Linette was about to end everything with him.

She gathered some courage and accepted his invitation. She, with her months of pregnancy, went to Hunter's apartment. The door was already open, she slightly pushed it away from her to find Hunter on his knees, holding a diamond ring. Her body froze. Her inner self cursed her for what she was about to do. She choked as she kept tears inside a cage.

'What's all this?' Linette's voice broke.

'I know I've been distant but! This is the reason why. I've been planning this forever now! Linette McCarthy will you be so kind as to accept this?' he asked with an innocent grin.

Two proposals in less than three months. Whether she liked it or not, she had to leave Hunter. She kept convincing herself that she was never right for him.

'I'm carrying Aaron's child.'
'What? Who's Aaron?' His grin disappeared.
'I've been with another man all this while—'
'Years of relationship or whatever we had—' his voice overlapped with Linette's.
'I'm sorry. Aaron and I are getting married next week.'
'When did you decide all of this? Who the fuck is Aaron? Please don't fool around like this.' His body was motionless, his heart beat faster than ever.
'Right after we... I can't, I'm sorry. I can't explain. I have to leave. I couldn't have ever asked you to take care of someone else's child with me. I always assumed you'd be better off without me.'
'Assumed?'
'Goodbye, Hunter.'

Without giving it a second thought, she exited his building with heavy tears. At that moment, she did not know what to think or what to say or how to put her feelings into words. Regardless of the outcome being good or bad, she knew she wasn't ready for either.

Hunter was left alone in a pond of his shattered respect. Things had radically changed in just a blink. His body froze on his knees as his shin started getting numb. Candles were flaming out and tears broke free. He watched Linette walk down an unknown path, entering a completely different life.

'Farewell, my friend.' He scoffed at his stupidity.

Chapter 7: Unknown

The human brain is absolutely crazy. It clearly knows what's right and what's wrong, yet it makes you do the latter. Ever wondered why? You see, if I keep an enclosed box in front of you, saying it carries a human head, and repeatedly ask you not to open it, what would you do? That's what I thought. If you think you wouldn't open it, reconsider. That little monster inside your head will let you know soon because there's a certain thrill in doing so. However, it is always followed by regret. Isn't it weird that it knows the consequence, yet it continues to violate? The fun part of the wrong eventually disappears and you finally realize that it is time to make things right. That is the human brain teaching you what life really looks like. Admit it already you've opened the box, haven't you?

It's a sunny day, the world is trying to heal itself. After the chaos, a silent atmosphere took over. Linette stood by the window, watching Hunter sit on her doorstep as he impatiently ripped off fresh grass from her lawn. A wall of guilt started to build in front of her eyes. It was hurtful to see him sit under that aggressive sun. She broke the wall and walked straight through it as she twisted the lock and held the door handle. Here goes nothing, she thought to herself.

She pulled the door inwards as he swiftly turned his face toward the creak of the hinge. He turned his vision back to the grass as he heard her sit beside him and sigh. They held their words inside for quite some time.

'B-bright day,' said Hunter, quietly.

'What could I have done differently?' Linette pressed her lips, recalling the past.

'To start off with, you could've not slept with another man, you could've left him instead not assuming that I would be a perfect fit for the child you carried… mine or not.'

'You deserved better.'

'Don't give me that crap, Lin—Mrs. O'Malley.'

'Linette is fine.' The tension in between them started disappearing. 'So, you didn't go out with anyone after that?'

'Why did you leave, Linette?'

'I was three months late with Aaron's child.'

'Two months,' he corrected her, throwing a suspicious look.

A loud noise interrupted their conversation. Their eyes caught Gracy harshly banging her fist against the window, from the inside of her house, succeeding in getting their attention. Hunter ran toward the house to find the door sealed from the outside. His hands expeditiously unlocked the door, whereas Eric briskly pulled it inwards.

'Where's Nathan?' Eric did not waste time.

'It's weird you ask me that, he wasn't home when I went there.' Hunter frowned. 'Found him shrieking on the streets.'

They revealed the secret of their awareness. As they kept explaining to Hunter about the messages from an unknown person, his eyes kept glancing at Linette's impatient wait across the street. 'Maybe we should show these to Mrs. O'Malley.'

They all agreed and strode toward Linette as her body showed restlessness. She was bewildered to see those messages. With every hapless thing around her, she walked toward her living room and settled down quietly. She waited; waited for something good to happen. Just as any situation was about to calm down, the universe would throw another alarming event at her.

'This person must be somewhere around us. I should go outside and' Hunter couldn't look for words in the midst of the chaos. Seeing Linette plonk herself to the couch, motionlessly, reminded him of the time when their parents had died. Before he could relive any of those moments, he rushed outside in search of someone he had never seen before.

Unexpectedly, not a lot of meters away, he saw a figure. The strong sun restricted his vision. The figure could be dancing around, and he wouldn't know. His right hand rested over his forehead only to reveal the figure pointing a gun, about to pull the trigger on him. Hunter's legs were paralyzed in horror. Sure, he wanted to run away, but time was cruel.

A bullet speed is around 2,500 feet per second and the processing speed of a normal human brain is 70 – 120 miles per second. I'd rather say we do not focus on math here. The brain is known for working involuntarily sometimes. What are the chances of it giving up on you when you need to decide something which would result in either life or death? Being at a gun point takes a lot of time to process that shit. Guess what? It's too late, the bullet has already pierced through his flesh.

A loud gunshot echoed in the silent streets of Annapolis. One moment, he was standing with his healthy body upright, the next he wasn't. Lying down in his own blood, seizing, Hunter was probably taking his last breath. The bullet had gone through his shoulder and he felt as if someone started reducing the brightness of his eyesight. He could feel his heart giving up on him. He was in excruciating pain.

The neighbors peeked out of their windows, just enough to see the shot-down body yet not in sight of any aggressive gunman. People broke free from Linette's house; however, she was being held by Sophia. Gracy pulled the bolt of her gun and pointed toward the bullet source, yet no one was in the range of her faculty of sight. Eric placed his three fingers on Hunter's neck to the side of his windpipe to pulse and felt a faint one. It was slowly decreasing.

Linette tried freeing herself from her unbreakable arms of Sophia. 'Please, Mrs. O'Malley, it's not safe outside!'

Linette blubbered and cried out loud. Her screams were audible till the far end of the street. 'Get him inside!' she yelled.

Gracy and Eric wrapped their arms on each of their shoulders and carefully walked toward Linette's house. Sophia made sure all the doors and windows were locked. She took the responsibility of guarding the house.

Hunter was placed on the rough beige carpet. His body was still, not a single muscle move was detected. Linette, with her unstable hands, put pressure on Hunter's wound. She was not ready to let go of another man. Her hyperventilation calmed down when she saw Samantha rush downstairs. 'Look away!'

'I heard a gunshot!'

'Sam! Go get the suturing kit I always talked about and place it on the stairs!' Linette ordered.

'Stay away from the windows and take care of Nate, OK?' Gracy added as she saw Samantha nod in agreement and run upstairs.

'Is there an exit wound?!' Linette yelled.

'There is,' Eric replied as he breathed through his mouth.

Linette took her time to look at Hunter's wound. 'It did not go through his artery.'

'Any damaged organ?'

'No.'

'How are you so sure?'

'I'm not.'

'Linette, suturing kit? Shouldn't we wait?' Gracy asked.

'I've done this before on animals.' Linette tried focusing, however, she felt her brain shutting down as she slowly watched Hunter pass out in her arms. She looked at him. 'Don't close your eyes, don't give up me there's so much left—'

Hunter replied with unintelligible words. All they could hear was his painful wheezing.

Samantha swiftly dropped the kit and ran upstairs, trying to avoid contact with the bleeding body. Gracy fetched it for Linette while hoping for the suturing to go well.

Linette took a breath and started the process. Why is this happening to me? She thought, while cautiously staring at her steady hands injecting the anesthesia inside his wound.

'Did you call an ambulance?'

Sophia replied in a low voice, 'All help lines are closed.'

Linette froze to concentrate on her breathing. She knew it was in her hands now. Not more than five seconds later, she watchfully continued with the medical care. Mid way through the stitching, all worried faces turned pale when they noticed Hunter's breathing coming to a stop. His eyes were shutting down, giving up.

'Hunter?' Gracy panicked.

Linette gasped and drew back her hands. 'OK,' she calmly let out those words. She handed over the heart needle and the Adson forceps to Eric, and wasting no time, pinched his nose and gave him mouth-to-mouth along with the Cardiopulmonary resuscitation. 1, 2, 3 two chest compressions and a firm blow in his mouth. It went on for quite a while, she hadn't given up yet.

'Maybe it's time to let go.' Sophia blunted out.

Linette ignored her and continued. Everyone else in the room had almost given up. A few minutes later, he opened his eyes and coughed, excruciatingly. However, he seemed better than before. His eyes were half-open as he playfully threw flirty looks at Linette.

Everyone beamed, whereas Sophia looked down in embarrassment. She might have spoken too soon. She felt witless.

'Linette,' Hunter tried talking through his parched throat.

Gracy lent Linette a bottle of water and watched Hunter distressingly gulp it down through Linette's hands.

'I think you should take him upstairs.' Gracy smiled at Hunter.

Linette looked at her and nodded in agreement. They took him upstairs, to her bedroom, along with his stabbing pain. The staircase was the hardest obstacle for him to overcome. After some time, his body was finally placed on the bed as it shivered with discomfort. A fever was rising up.

Linette sat down beside him and continued stitching up his wound. 'You might feel a pinch.' She said platonically while watching Hunter wince in pain.

Downstairs.

Gracy received a new message. 'Just when you thought things were getting better.' She nodded and sighed in frustration.

'You think it was him?' Eric asked, furiously looking outside the window.

'This unknown guy?' She scoffed. 'He's just some ordinary man, he couldn't have done it.'

A message followed the previous one. 'I know who did it.' Gracy read it out loud.

Eric snatched the phone from her hand. They had it enough, it was time to reveal the unknown face. 'OK, who was it?' He sent a message.

The reply did not take a lot of time to arrive. 'One of your own—Maverick Miller.'

'It wasn't him.' Eric knew the mind games the person had been playing, he wasn't dumb enough to fall for them again.

'I see you're studying my behavior, impressive. Fine, it wasn't Maverick. Officer Gomez.'

Eric chose not to reply back. Instead, he looked at Gracy and asked, 'He's saying it' s Gomez. Is he capable of—'

Gracy shrugged her shoulders and frowned. 'He was on duty near this street and apparently was not answering his radio. I recognized the bullet I found near Hunter's body, these don't sell easily to common people. It could be Gomez, but why would he do that?'

'What if he was one of those? People are still turning into rotters.' Eric searched for a word as he watched Gracy's frown get more wrinkled.

'Huh? Rotters?'

'Well, Dr. Campbell said that their bodies were sort of rotting, so I just gave them a name I guess.'

Gracy shook her head in despair. She ordered Sophia to check on the updates with the number that her team had been tracking down. 'Get me that person.' She was infuriated.

With her gifted memory, Sophia dialed Poppy's number on the telephone. The team had been working hard in order to trace the person down. With everything piling up, it was getting difficult for them to handle the madness.

'Sophia!' Jacob yelled from far away. 'Come to the department now!'

'Yes, sir.' Sophia cut the call and calmed herself down. She looked at Gracy and politely took her permission to leave. Gracy permitted, without considering the means of transport she would use to get there.

'Call us when you reach,' Eric added.

'Certainly.' Sophia smiled and exited the house. Her frightened feet somehow managed to walk out in the open as she faintly heard growling noises. *Maybe it's just your brain playing games with you,* she consoled herself.

At the police station.

Poppy and Jacob never enjoyed each other's company. They can't come up with nice things to say to, or about, each other. None of them bothered to even exchange a friendly smile. Jacob always reminded Poppy of an emotionless robot. Whereas the robot himself had an indifferent view of her. Neither of them was really excited about working on the number together. Every time Poppy failed to track it down, he looked at her and scoffed out loudly, making her want to end his existence.

'Poppy, funny name you've got there. P-O-P-P-Y,' he taunted.

'You are best at testing my patience.' She had given up on tracing the number.

'No, I'm just—'

'You think after saving me back there you'll earn my respect?'

'What are you talking about?'

'Opening the gates was my doing, we both know that! You tried to stop me and maybe that's exactly why I opened them because boy, do I love disrespecting your silly little commands! Why did you take the blame? To later on brag to

Gracy and the others about your heroic moment? To rub it on my face? If you think I owe you anything after this, you're expecting too much.'

'I did not do that for anything else but to save your ass from getting more humiliated than you already were!'

Poppy focused on the screen, blankly.

At Linette's place.

Linette succeeded in patching him up neatly, and Hunter looked better. Her eyes followed the trails of blood on her white top.

'Sorry about that,' he whispered in a thick voice.

'This? Oh, don't be. This top's too old anyway.'

'Linette, what were you trying to say about there being so much left? What's left?'

'I was just blabbing nonsense to keep you awake.'

'Perfect, so there's nothing left?'

'Don't speak to me as if we've been close for years.'

'But we have, have we not?'

'My husband is dead, Hunter.'

Silence took over. Tree branches started tapping against the window. Hunter pressed his lips and sealed his confrontation. Leaving him in the room, Linette left. He had never felt such a strong Deja Vu until that very moment.

Downstairs.

The person behind the screen was feeling guilty for what had happened. After the bullet pierced through Hunter's shoulder, the unknown put a stop to playing games with them and finally decided to have a face reveal. 'I have answers to your questions. Stay put, I'm coming. And don't you dare point a gun at me, you people do that a lot.'

Eric looked at Gracy skeptically. She kept her phone aside and looked back at him. 'Is this safe?' Eric questioned.

Gracy shrugged her shoulders. 'No weapons involved.'

'He's bluffing—' A patient doorbell interrupted their conversation.

They looked at each other and ran toward it. He twisted the lock and pulled the door. Gracy stood behind, trying to peek through Eric's broad shoulders. She had already created an image of the character from the phone. According to her, it was a young man with long, rough hair. He had dusky skin and embraced his worn-out clothes.

But to her shock, the person on her doorstep was someone they would have never pictured.

A gorgeous young lady, in her youth. Even the filthy green gown looked pretty on her gorgeous curvy body. Her dark brown eyes sparkled with playfulness. Her shoulder-length, pitch-black hair flew along with the wind breeze.

'I'm sorry, who are you?' Eric seemed confused. Did she walk into the wrong house? Was she lost? He completely kept aside the fact that it could be the unknown who brought uttermost chaos into their lives.

The girl smirked at him. 'I see you weren't expecting a lady.'

Chapter 8: Fenjiyawa

Stories. We all love stories and the drama that goes on; however, we hate drama when we are involved in the story.

"I belong to the land and waters of Fenjiyawa, my motherland. The land you people invaded. I'm sure you've barely heard about this island; we've been able to live in the shadows all this while. You see, it's quite far away from the real world. Not that people there lived in absolute ignorance, just that we are far better and civilized than you nincompoops. ' We' as in the Fenjees. I've never seen it, but people tell me how joyful the island was, not even one sad element was found. It was so beautiful that the Fenjees were selfish to share it with the outside, cruel world. Who can blame them? Doesn't take time for you people to destroy something so beautiful, so pure.

I've spent enough time here to explore your entire arena and I have happened to come across the legend of Nicodemus the tenth. The book says: Aristarchus was a weak ruler and Nicodemus rescued the king—mother nature! I can't even complete this sentence without feeling disgusted. You people think Aristarchus was… what did your friend say? A piece of shit? What utter crap your world sells; the writer must be a nincompoop.

I am a descendant of that family, Aristarchus was no weak, he was no threat to the community. Huh, but your mankind got the virus section right, the master project we are not quite thrilled about.

Every bit was as normal as the outside world, so they say. Except for one thing—the Fenjees were cannibals to the outsiders. Many of a person used to sail to the "mysterious island" and never made it back to the real world. That is because the Fenjees used to hunt them down and have them for supper. They say humans are tasty. Fear not, I wouldn't know. I somehow became an herbivore. Tourists, wanderers, reporters, all gone. You see, Fenjees belong to a community where we come in peace, that is until our privacy is invaded—the land is our privacy. So, once you step into Fenjiyawa, there is no going back alive. Our land was beautiful alright, but we all know what this world does to these untainted beauties.

It all started in the year 1819, Fenjiyawa's following leader was born, Aristarchus the eleventh—whose great grandfather, we believe, had found the island. Bravery and kindness ran in his blood. He began to rule the kingdom by 1869. He had a boy looking up to him and who was next in line for the throne. This was taken away from him when a large number of people with double ammunition invaded our land. He called himself Nicodemus the ninth. He was an actual king from another island trying to conquer more. Fenjiyawa was his last stop.

You'd think they had a war? No sire. Nicodemus adored competitions. He challenged Aristarchus's son with a simple preference box. Yes, a preference box, shocking. People of all ages had the freedom to vote for their preferred representatives. You'd also think the Fenjees unquestionably would've voted for Aristarchus, right? Wrong again. Fenjees like thrilling experiences, they like people with more ammunition I guess we're not as civilized as we thought. In their defense, this Nicodemus guy sounded a little manipulative to me.

Fortunately, only for him of course, he was crowned as the new king. A huge turn of events for Fenjiyawa. I'll not waste anyone's valuable time by telling how the kingdom was taken over. All I know is he was a good ruler at first, but slowly, made Fenjiyawa a living hell. He increased Fenjees' working hours, with very little reward. He took away everyone's children. He believed and made everyone believe that if a child was sacrificed, more wealth would knock on their door, and so he did. He sacrificed a lot of children. He went deranged.

He banished the Aristarchus family and their true followers. He took away all the palaces they owned, all the money they had, all the will they possessed, and then built a wall in between them and the kingdom. When I say wall, don't get your hopes high, it was only a bamboo wall.

Aristarchus the eleventh lost all his good and polite qualities—who wouldn't? The Nicodemus family came out of nowhere and took over the entire land. What does a man want now? Revenge. He did not want to show any kind of mercy on the king and his people, no matter what they were going through. They brought this upon themselves, right? They shouldn't have voted for him in the first place.

'There will be no kingdom if he does not have any sane people to rule upon.' His words are still alive. These words started an insurrection.

Aristarchus the eleventh was a crazy scientist. Yes, can you imagine? He planned on creating a virus that would make people lose themselves, they wouldn't possess any control over their brains, and they would get violent and hurt their own loved ones. It took him five years to prepare for the virus. He kicked the bucket before he could implement his ideas. The creation of the virus was passed on to Aristarchus the twelfth like he was passed the baton. He was unmindful of what the virus was going to do, he only knew revenge.

They grew an herb named Zerm that activated the virus. Hence, the name—Zermaitus. The paper had clear instructions—one handful of Zerm. The twelfth went ruthless and added four instead. Boy, was he so keen on destroying the entire kingdom. Let's just skip all this and go straight to where he died. The legacy was then carried on by his sons—Emanuel and Inhune. The virus-making was unstoppable.

And finally, they were successful in creating the virus. You want drama? Fenjiyawa had them too! Inhune fell in love with someone—Abiyeth, and so did Emanuel—Abiyeth. Same lady. Don't ask me how and why but she first carried Emanuel's child, a boy, and then a year later, Inhune's child, a girl. She didn't know who she was falling for. But enough with the love triangle. The trio wasn't distracting anyone.

Coming back to the virus the brothers had complete access to the kingdom, they made a secret tunnel, and were successful in secretly injecting the virus into the main grain storage that was accessible to all Fenjees. Their furiousness led them to empty the entire bottle of the virus into their food. They waited and waited, and slowly, the Fenjees started getting sick. They observed all this stealthily. They saw they were disturbed and frustrated with their lives, and many of them tried killing themselves too. They were jolly to see them suffer. However the very next day, they heard weird, loud grunting noises from the kingdom side and they were shocked. People were tearing off each other's flesh, parents killing and eating their own offspring, people just going out of their bloody minds! Nature turned dark and gloomy.

The brothers started panicking. They found an antidote—a grayish-green flower Aristarchus freely grew in his backyard. And of course, they called it Fenjaitus. I'm embarrassed with the names they've kept but it is what it is.

They squeezed out all the syrup from Fenjaitus and injected it to every exiled side. Remember I said don't get your hopes high? Yeah, people from the other side started breaking the wall.

Just as everyone's anticipation was washed out, a boat sailed toward them two nincompoops all merry about finding an island. The moment the boat reached the shore, the Fenjees slaughtered the mariners—no big deal there. Only two people could leave the island. Inhune was generous enough to let Abiyeth and Emanuel take their son and leave. Of course, the only deal was that they would come back with more help.

'Emanuel! We're counting on you, do come back,' Inhune yelled to them, watching them move away from the island, to safer land.
'I will come back, brother. You have my word, brother!' Emanuel yelled back.
'Praise all-mother!' everyone exclaimed.

The crazy infected ones made it to the exiled side. The Fenjees, under the leadership of Inhune, put forth their brawn and fought. The first war of Fenjiyawa. Putting all their lives into it, they succeeded in trapping all the infected ones in their little nets. Let's just say that the exiled side won and nothing ever threatened them.

Years passed by; people struggled. Emanuel and Abiyeth never came back. Maybe they found a high tide and vanished into the waves, or maybe they were just selfish after all. Fenjees were wishing they were dead, not as a curse, but they hoped that it was the only explanation for them not returning.

A few more years passed by, and betrayal killed Inhune. They found him cold on his bed. They say he died peacefully. People are fading away without a leader. There's not enough food, not enough greenery, not enough strength.'

The room was silent. Gracy and Eric were speechless. What could have they asked? Everything was so clearly placed in front of them. Her story was so unimaginable that the winds stopped blowing, trees shed their leaves and the sun hid behind gray clouds. Throats were dry, not a word was left to utter.

'When your people came in search of this Island,' the woman continued. 'They opened all the cages we built for the infected ones—don't know why we still kept them around. I was just near the shore when it all happened, calming myself down, and then a ship stopped by. I thought we were being saved. I snuck myself into the ship and loitered around a little. I heard their conversations. They weren't there to help us, they were there to invade us. They immediately sailed off, leaving me no choice but to stay back in the ship and go with the flow, quite literally with the waves."

'You're one of the Fenjees?' Gracy whispered in a low voice, never thinking she would ask such a nonsensical question to anyone.

'I'm the one Abiyeth left behind. Inhune's daughter. Erica Aristarchus.'

Chapter 9: Untold

The human brain... spoiled. Even when the truth is beautifully presented to them on a fancy platter, they won't believe a thing. Denying reality is its favorite hobby, but who can blame them? People usually cannot take the amount of pressure after what has been unraveled to them. However, you cannot expect life to give you something you wouldn't be able to handle, can you?

Linette stood near the partially opened door, staring at Hunter. She took a long breath and entered the room, knowing she would have to face his questions.

'You always come back,' said a hoarse voice.

Linette popped out a pain killer from the packet and poured him a glass of water.

'Linette,' he tried to talk.

She slammed the glass on the table and roughly placed the pill in his palm. 'Can you let go?' She could not stand breathing in the same room as him, even though she knew that her doing was wrong. Her reckless and destroyed brain punished Hunter. She headed out of the room until these few words stopped her from doing so.

'Samantha's eyes are green,' said he.

'What?' She turned around and found Hunter holding a family frame that was placed on the table, right beside the bed.

'Your eyes are pure hazel. Aaron's eyes are gray. Oh, Nathan has his mother's eyes! Samantha and I have the exact same color.' Hunter clenched his teeth while watching her exit the room.

Downstairs.

It was like the moment after an exhausting hurricane. No, there was no rainbow, just a little break from the disaster.

Eric looked at Erica. 'I don't want to believe in your story.'

She rolled up her sleeves to reveal a mark. It was an unknown language enclosed in a perfect circle. It was the mark imprinted onto Fenjees' arms after injecting them with the antidote. 'I have the protection.' She pulled her already wrinkled cloth to show them a human bite. It was a torn flesh that was healing with time. 'It's been two years. I'm still me. The bite didn't affect me in any way.'

'Gracy?' Eric whispered. The mark was familiar.

Gracy gasped and looked at Eric with wide eyes. She remembered looking at a similar mark on his arm. Eric raised his arm to compare them. They matched. He was disquieted. The glimpse of the mark on his hand pushed Erica back as she inhaled sharply. It gave her a jolt.

'You're Eric Aristarchus?' Erica stared at him while holding her head in disbelief.

'My mother used to shut me down every time I asked her about this,' Eric recalled.

'You're Eric Aristarchus,' Erica repeated.

'No,' he whispered, 'I'm an Ainsworth! This is a setup! What do you want from us?'

'This imprint was created by Aristarchus—'

'Shut up, you!'

Gracy was quiet throughout their conversation. She felt her brain trying to process everything, and it had all lined up. There was no other possible explanation for what was going on. And it felt relieving to believe that Eric had the vaccine running in his blood, protecting him from the virus. 'Eric was scratched by an infected man.'

'He's not going to be sick.' Erica nodded, trying to convince them.

'I have the vaccine?' Eric frowned, taking a second look at his mark.

'With that imprint, you most certainly do.'

'How did you find me?'

'I did not. The universe brought me to you.'

Upstairs.

Linette clutched the green lens case in her palm and entered the room. Hunter moved his eyes away from her as she walked closer to him.

'What?' asked Hunter as he slightly nodded his head.

'You wanna know why her eyes are green in this frame?'

'Why?'

She took a long breath and threw the lens case on his motionless body. 'She loves wearing these.'

Hunter was embarrassed. He felt silence would make it more awkward, so he chose his words right by spilling his heart. 'I'm sorry, Linette. I'm going crazy. Everything hurts and I guess I needed to share my burden with someone. It shouldn't be you.'

'Strange times.'

'Hm.' Except for his strange times started when Linette walked out of his life.

She left the room mid-conversation, holding a mysterious guilt of proving Hunter wrong, and decided to step down stairs. She was unaware of the new face she would be meeting.

She looked at Erica and smiled at her thoughtfully. The stubborn lady replied with zero facial movements. Linette raised her eyebrows and looked at Gracy to introduce them. She held her phone up high. Linette was smart enough to pick up that hint. 'You mean the one who broke into my house and took my child?' A slightly aggressive tone took over.

'I apologize for my unethical actions and offer you my remorse.' Erica got up and put her hand forward, 'Erica Aristarchus.'

Linette shook her hand. 'Linette O'Malley.' She looked at G racy and asked, 'Why am I greeting her?'

Erica withdrew her hand, 'I am from the island your loved one went to.' Linette's face turned pale, she fidgeted with her dress as everything around her became mum to her ears.

On the other hand, Eric's brain couldn't stop processing. Eric and Erica, parents weren't quite creative with our names. Is this really a coincidence or is she trying to trick us? I shouldn't trust her too soon.

The questions were endless, he surely did want to believe in everything Erica had revealed, however, it felt unreal to him. And why wouldn't it? Santa Claus sounded more real than Erica's mysterious island.

'Are you really my sister?' Eric interrupted the silent room.

'Adding a vowel at the end of your name makes it my name,' Erica replied.

'Sister?' Linette was done with all the new events coming up. She did not know what to feel, how to feel, or when to grieve. The universe was successful in making her an emotionless robot.

In different circumstances, Gracy wanted answers and she needed them soon enough to save Annapolis from the virus. 'Since you already know a lot about what is happening, Erica, how do we stop this virus from spreading?'

Erica looked at Gracy. 'Oh.' she laughed. 'There is no way.'

'There is always a way.'

'There's no stopping this, until—'

'I will go to any extent.'

'Until we sail back to Fenjiyawa and get the vaccine.'

Chapter 10: Unclear Paths

The sun had set, the number of cases had increased and the jolly environment had deceased. There was nothing but terror in the air, not a single person dared to walk on the streets of Annapolis. There was only one channel on the television that repeated a warning.

This is not a drill. Stay indoors until further notice. Lock and barricade all the doors and windows. Do not try to reach for your loved ones. In case of an emergency call 18000, all the other lines have been shut down. To ensure safety, every street is guarded by a police officer. Any suspicious events must be reported to them. We request you to stay calm and not panic. Thank you.

People looked out of their windows to find officers guarding the roads with loaded ammunition. They were not sure if they were to feel safe or more unsafe. Gunshots were heard far away from the residential areas. However, as time passed by, they started getting closer and clearer. Every house on the streets had sleepless nights with frightening thoughts. 'Zombies do not exist. It's fake news, they can't be real.' People consoled themselves.

Scientists and investigators were being interviewed from Annapolis and nearby cities. These interviews were all over the radio channels.

'Most of the scientists do believe that Zombies can be created of course, it won't be as dramatic as shown in the movies,' said Dr. Capshaw, a scientist from Chester.

'Y-yes we do believe that some viruses have control over the brain. In fact, there are plenty of viruses out there that can make one very aggressive but you can't simply call it a Zombie apocalypse, that's just absurd,' said another scientist from Mayo.

'What we are dealing with is umm impassive. They have no other function but to create destruction. They feed on things that a normal human being simply just don't,' said Maverick in his interview with Annapolis's Radio station.

'Dr. Maverick, how much time will it take to create the vaccine?' asked the interviewer.

'Normally, it would take around 18 months. But forget about the vaccine, we haven't even discovered the virus yet. The investigation is ongoing and we won't stop until we get to the bottom of this.'

'Thank you, Dr. Maverick. We have another famous pathologist from Annapolis, Dr. Raghav Campbell. Doctor, many people out there are convinced that this is a Zombie apocalypse. What are your views on this theory?' The interviewer put forth her question.

'Zombies? We say that nonsense because of what television has taught us. I refuse to believe in this theory, you should too. I know this, for sure, that if we do not find a cure soon enough, this virus might slowly spread to the entire country and will result in a second pandemic.'

'Do you think we can find a cure soon enough?'

'No, not when I am here giving answers to you.' Dr. Campbell abruptly cut the line.

'Uh, apologies for that. As we can see, all our doctors and scientists are certainly looking into this, without wasting any valuable time. These were the interviews with the topmost scientists and investigators. The advice from them is to quarantine yourselves and if possible, barricade your doors and windows. Singing off, RJ Millie Wilson hopefully, until next time.'

A high-pitched frequency was heard which was followed by a warning.

'This is not a dri—' Linette turned off the radio and looked at everyone with great apprehension.

'Was it just me or did everyone hear the interviewer call Maverick a doctor because he's certainly not. How did he get them to do that?' Eric wondered.

'We have to alert the health authorities.' Gracy sighed gently. 'They have no clue what this is.'

'We keep it that way,' Erica added. 'Fenjiyawa shall remain a secret.'

'So we leave them clueless? Is this a joke? Watching them struggle with the answers? Sooner or later, they'll get to the index patient and will question the island.' Eric looked at her with fury.

'The vaccine has already been created.' Erica stayed calm.

'Why do we believe you?' asked Gracy, tiredly.

'You will when we go to Fenjiyawa,' Erica answered.

'I guess we'll never know because we are certainly not going there,' Eric interrupted. He refused to believe in someone who had just walked into their lives. 'We'll tell them what it is and they'll find a cure to it.'

'There is!' Erica lowered her voice as she felt she was louder than usual, 'There is a cure to it already.'

'What will guarantee our safety? You said they were cannibals to the outsiders.' Gracy put forth a few questions before accepting the plan.

'I am the guarantee!'

'We can't leave everyone in the dark. We also can't go there unprepared.'

Erica nodded her head unenthusiastically.

'Roger has the right to know everything about Fenjiyawa.'

'Why?' asked Erica.

'He's the only survivor, he should know what it was. Besides, he could arrange the same ship for us.'

Erica sat upright, 'We don't require him.'

'Do you know any captain who will be willing to help us reach there? Because none of us do.'

Erica stared at her and deeply inhaled. 'One person, no one else.'

The three of them decided to visit Roger. Eric looked at Linette and handed her a pocket knife. 'Take care of Hunter.'

'Why does it sound like you're asking me to kill him?'

'I studied the actions the moment I did it, my apologies. Barricade the door if possible.'

'Alright.' Linette gulped in fear, knowing she wouldn't be able to handle any more alarming situations.

Gracy insisted on driving, Eric called shotgun. He turned his face toward the back of the car, where Erica was fidgeting with the leather seats. Unknowingly, his body had completely turned in the direction of her presence. He smooshed his cheek on the headrest and stared at her till she felt the need to address it.

'Stop ogling, you weird human!' She watched him get a sudden jerk of realization. His stare had gotten too evident.

Gracy looked at Erica through the rear-view mirror with a smile. 'He's looking for resemblance.'

'We don't look similar.' Eric frowned.

'We have different fathers.' Erica rolled her eyes.

'Why me?' Eric turned back to the empty road and crossed his arms.

'Yeah, why you? You look like someone straight out of a garbage can.' Erica, too, folded her arms and pushed herself back against the seat.

'I see the resemblance,' Gracy murmured as she concentrated on her driving.

'Speaking of fathers, where is Emanuel?' Erica asked, curiously.

'His name is Edgar now. He's with my mother, our mother—Abigail now. They're in Frederick, an hour away.'

'It's fine, you can keep your mother to yourself. Do they know I'm here?'

'No.'

Gracy rolled her car to a stop. They clambered from the car and strode toward Roger's door. She knocked on the door with her firm knuckles. 'Open up, Roger!'

No one answered it. While Gracy and Eric took a step back to look through the open window, Erica twisted the door handle and pushed the door inward .

'That's trespassing!' yelled Gracy in a hushed voice.

'Trespassing was entering Fenjiyawa.' Erica's stern voice took over.

Eric raised his eyebrows and turned to Gracy. 'I see the resemblance too now.'

Chapter 11: Join Us

Nature had quietened down. The birds who chirped every morning were silenced by the entity. Trees that used to dance along with the winds, were standing still. Dry leaves were dragged along the road and the sound that it created was the only sound heard by all. The warnings had increased. Scientists were failing as people started fading away from Earth. They were helpless. Not even one eye could be rested without fearing the virus. There were hardly any guards left to double the protection; not many were determined enough to face these deadly creatures, largely known as homo sapiens.

'We're not permitted to go in,' Gracy whispered. 'Don't.'

Erica, staying in her character, pushed the door wide open while peeling off her dry chapped lips with her teeth, till she could taste blood. As the door was wide enough for a person to go through, Erica looked at Eric, asking him to be the first one to step into the dark rusty house.

He rolled his eyes and tiptoed inside, cautiously. As they took two steps further against the creaking wood, he suddenly put a stop to his legs to point out a shadow.

They saw a silhouette of a man who stood on the other side of the wall with a raised weapon. Gracy rested her hand on her pocket gun and called him out from the other side, her eyes focused on every move the man-made.

'Roger? It's me, Officer Brown. Put down your weapon.'

The shadow's hands did as it was asked to. Gracy relaxed her hand and casually walked toward the shadow. To everyone's shock, the shade's face did not reveal Roger. It was a man who possessed an angry face as his blood tried to rush into the sclera and paint it red. He was preparing to pounce on anybody that appeared to be in front of him.

As Gracy tried to throw herself away, the man held her neck tightly with a clear motive to kill her. Eric did his best to separate his love from the ruthless swine. He powerfully punched the man twice. On getting the second punch, the man lost his balance and fell to the ground, still very determined to get up and choke Gracy to death.

Erica reached out for Gracy's gun and shot a bullet through the man's head as blood splattered all over the ground. This was just another diseased body for them. The guilt of not feeling guilty, however, did take place.

'Quick thinking.' Gracy hyperventilated as she hunched and held her knees, not knowing whether Erica's actions were ethical or not.

Erica turned the gun toward a gasp, coming from the stairs.

'Don't shoot! It's me, Roger!' he exclaimed with his trembling hands up in the air. Knowing not every move Erica made was a smart one, Eric snatched the gun from her hand. He kept the gun back to where it belonged and slightly touched Gracy's neck, 'Does it hurt?'

Gracy nodded and turned to Roger. 'Care to join us?'

Roger crept downstairs as his body shivered, staring disgustedly at the dead man. Somehow, he was doing just fine for someone who had a dead body lying on an ancient carpet that seemed very expensive.

Erica scratched her head. 'Sorry about your pal here. He wasn't being so nice.'

Roger looked at her with a frown as he took the last step. 'I don't know who he is. He snuck into my house a few minutes ago and seemed very aggressive— I haven't seen so much anger in anyone before. He looked very ready to smash anyone's head with that ax of his, so I quietly locked myself into my room, praying for help, and then I heard a gunshot. Thank you, I guess.'

'My pleasure, I could do this all day.'

'Erica,' Eric whispered and turned his face toward her, scared of her confidence in man slaughtering.

They put the body aside and sat down on the vintage brown sofa which seemed very uncomfortable. 'My therapist said it's best to stand in such situations.' Erica strolled around the house and admired the prehistoric wall hangings.

'I doubt there are therapists on an island,' Gracy whispered to Eric.

'The couch is uncomfortable.' Eric whispered back, watching her nod in agreement.

The story of Fenjiyawa began its journey, yet again, as Gracy carefully placed all the events in front of Roger. Only listening to the word "Fenjiyawa" made Roger's jaw clench as the memory attached to that island triggered a fresh wound.

Just when he thought he would never get any nearer to that island, he was asked to risk his life and enter the catastrophic hands of Fenjiyawa, again.

'Do you know what you're asking me to do? And don't even tell me that you understand because you don't! I lost everything to that island and you want me to go back?' Roger started breathing with great difficulty, through his trembling lips.

'We won't be able to do this without you.' Gracy knew taking him along was not the right thing, however, he was the bridge between Annapolis and Fenjiyawa.

'Am I being used here? F-for the connections I have with the captain of the ship?'

'OK, we know he's your brother.'

'Way to go, officer.'

'I know things were complicated between you two, and that's why we didn't question you related to why you never told anyone that you had someone from your family staying in Annapolis. But even you know that only you can convince him to get us there. He wouldn't do it if you're not on that ship risking your life with him, would he? That's why he agreed in the first place. You'll be given a good reward for this by the department.'

Roger sat there, motionless. His brain processed her words. As soon as he did, he sighed and laughed. 'So I *am* being used here.'

'Is he?' Eric looked at Gracy with disappointment. He realized she was never concerned with Roger knowing the story of Fenjiyawa but to get to the island. To his reply, Gracy nodded and assured that her intentions were good—they always had been.

A loud thud against the window interrupted their conversation. Their eyes witnessed a woman running into it, trying to get to them and hurting herself in the process. It was as if she was unaware of the transparent shield that separated her from the people inside.

The demented woman's arms were barely hanging from her body. The pungent smell of her oozing blood with thick sticky yellow liquid reached everyone's lungs, through the walls. She looked at them furiously and kept banging the glass with her closed, weak fist till blood splashed all over the window.

'Make her stop!' Roger closed his eyes and covered his ears as he whimpered.

'Make me!' yelled the woman from the other side. The glass started creating small cracks, till she could break through, Erica rushed toward the door and locked herself outside with the infected.

'You know it's taking control over you, right?' Erica casually placed herself in front of the woman.

'You have real nerves coming out here.' The woman's sinister voice overlapped Erica's, as her mouth spat blood in the air. She seemed to have two personalities, the real she was fighting to come out. 'I know it's controlling me,' She cried hysterically.

Erica stood there, watching the woman limping closer to her, asking to end her life. However, the virus overpowered her voice and her motive changed. Laughing frantically, she prepared herself to pounce on Erica.

The moment froze for Fenjiyawa's lass. A wave of current rushed into her veins and gave her the chills. It was the moment of realization that the real world needed the vaccine more than ever. Her ambience was interrupted by a gunshot that went straight through the woman's head.

'Are you out of your mind? She was going to kill you.' Gracy shook Erica, realizing the fact that she was no more hesitant to kill.

'We need to get to Fenjiyawa.' They went back inside. Erica stood by the window, trying to look away from the innocent woman's pale contorted body that stared back at her.

Roger gulped, he sat down on the couch as his shivery hands searched for the arm rest. He nodded slowly and gathered the courage to let out these words. 'He would risk his life if I'm in it too. Just get these bodies away from my eyesight.'

'We'll take care of it, but you're going to have to tag along with us from now on.' Gracy watched Roger's face muscles relax back to their original position. 'Eric, tell me we don't have to involve our teams.'

'They're already involved,' he replied, hating that he had to drag everyone on this dangerous expedition.

'That doubles the number of lives at risk.' Erica nodded.

'A single stick can snap easily, a bunch of them can't.'

'Well, Fenjiyawa is a guillotine—will cut right through the bunch of them.'

'Then none of us should be going.'

'The more the merrier.' Not letting any displeased words out, her quick smile turned into an eye roll.

It was time for Gracy to involve her team in the plan. She went through her contacts in search of Poppy—a name that stood out on her list. However, with the objectives running in her mind, her eyes couldn't catch her name. Saving her the trouble, Poppy's name took over the screen. She frowned and picked up the call to an excited voice.

Poppy started brightly informing, 'We found the man to that unknown number! A business tycoon who visits Annapolis only once a year. He's in custody right now, says his phone was stolen lying bas—'

'Poppy! About that'

'You don't sound very impressed.'

'This is something I should have informed you, officers, way back.' Gracy laughed nervously.

'Grace?'

'He's not lying, the phone was stolen. Long story short—' Gracy continued Erica's story, leaving the officers rather amazed. 'It's alarming, I know. We need the vaccine. I am only going to ask this once, Fenjiyawa—in or out?'

'Right now, what could be worse than this place anyway?'

'The place where it all began.'

'You have our assistance.'

'Good, meet me at my place in about an hour, with the entire team, but leave Sophia out of it.'

'I thought she was already with you.'

'Didn't she stop by the station? She left in a hurry when Jacob yelled at her,' Gracy replied, trying to recall the incident.

'She did not.' Poppy looked at Jacob, confused.

'Find her, and do something about the bodies at Roger's place—don't ask.'

'Wasn't gonna.' Poppy slammed the phone in front of Jacob. 'Sophia's missing.' Her silent, but very evident blame added to his self-inculpating pile. He quietly suffered guilt.

At Roger's place.

Gracy looked at Erica and scratched her head. 'It just doesn't make sense. All this while we've been thinking they're Zombies, and from what I know Zombies don't talk. That lady Zombie spoke to you, right?'

'Zombies?' Erica chuckled. 'What a silly name. Proves that you people hate them.' She clicked her tongue. 'If you didn't question them while they were slaughtering and eating each other, why question something every human being already does?'

'The real world is way more messed up than you think,' Eric added.

'I'm sure it is.' Looking at Eric engrossed in his phone, she approached him personally and meandered around him.

'Is there something you need?' Eric noticed her obvious presence.

Erica nodded and replied, 'You haven't told your parents, have you?'

'I haven't, but they're on their way here. It'll be best if you don't startle them. Let me do the talking, OK?'

'You do the talking.' Erica smiled as a mischievous plan started building behind her mind.

Roger marched downstairs with a brown briefcase—the only polished and well-maintained commodity that he possessed. Showing his face for the last time to his house, he announced, 'Let's go before I change my mind.'

Chapter 12: Regained Daughters

Lying is the most demanding accomplishment of the human brain. These decisions are taken by an electric simulation of the prefrontal cortex. That was too much science for a chapter! Let's just conclude that lying is easy. Imagine if a human is capable of fooling a polygraph test, how effortless will it be to lie to another human being. As long as you believe in your own lie, the truth is locked away forever. But what happens when you fail to believe it?

Annapolis and its nearing cities were on a lockdown—no one could enter or exit these premises. The virus outbreak had infected many brains. Detecting it was impossible as people who were the carriers wouldn't come in hand very easily. The only way to stop the infected ones from running away was to shoot a bullet through their brains.

At Gracy's house.

The teams were functioning under a single thought—getting the vaccine. This journey didn't seem to be an easy one. To get to Fenjiyawa, they would have to sneak out of the city, which would be near impossible with the ship they were going to board. Not to mention the diseased people waiting for them on the island, they needed weapons, they needed a fully-fledged plan.

Everyone convened at Gracy's, trying to find the best route for Fenjiyawa. They spread themselves in the living room as Gracy prepared them for the secret mission. Her eyes wandered, watching the busy room, but stopped as they witnessed Jacob's solitary.

'When was the last time I saw you sitting in the corner, doing nothing?' Gracy walked toward Jacob. 'Never,' she answered her own question.

Jacob scoffed. 'Sophia left the house because of me, I pushed her around too much, and now she's missing.'

Gracy chose silence as a reply.

Linette sat downstairs, on her couch, drowned in deep thoughts. She finally found a chance to grieve. How unfortunate must be a person who is constantly looking for an opportunity to mourn. Hunter and the kids were asleep—it was the perfect time to remember the dead. She closed her eyes and pleasantly smiled as her brain showed her a montage of Aaron and their memories together. As time passed by, she felt her muscles taking a break, her heart was beating normally again.

She opened her eyes and glanced at a frame as her reflection stared back at her tears. It took her back to the day when Nathan had seen his first shark. Aaron and Samantha broke into laughter as the little boy cried thinking the shark would get to him—Linette found the most beautiful moment to capture.

Her body was at peace until she heard someone descending downstairs. She wasn't disturbed by the noise; her grieving was eventually going to have an end to it. She stared at the empty staircase, discerning who it could be. The footsteps were heavy, it wasn't her children's. The legs stopped to let out a soft grunt.

'Hunter?' Linette called out blindly. On getting no reply, she carefully rose from her couch and chose her weapon—Nathan's baseball bat. The pocketknife seemed too violent. She grabbed the bat and crouched beside the staircase. 'Hunter.' She gave another chance for a descending body to speak. Reply to her voice was a louder grunt. As the legs started creeping down the stairs again, she saw a man's feet that had blood dripping on them. Linette closed her eyes and aimlessly threw the baseball bat toward the growl, with great force. The body was successful in dodging the bat, but the sudden movement brought itself two steps down.

'Linette!' Hunter shrieked in pain.

'Hunter?'

'Psycho! What is wrong with you?'

'Do you always have to creep up on me like that?'

'Why do you have all these panic moves ready to go?'

'You groaned like a Zombie!'

'I heard you call out my name, so I tried replying but this stupid pain is taking over my voice so stop making me talk!' Hunter rambled out loud as he kept his hand on the railing.

Linette ran half way upstairs to help him get down. 'You need a re-dress on that wound.' She watched his blood dripping from the open wound.

The noise got the kids' attention. On hearing their doorknob, Linette slightly pushed Hunter away from their sight. Watching a man bleed wouldn't be a great vision to Samantha. She wasn't so worried about Nathan—tell the boy the man dipped in a raspberry fondue and he would believe it.

Hunter could balance the slight push for a few seconds but eventually, fell to the ground. Linette's jaw dropped after watching the heavy fall. Her lips fought that reaction with a smile as her children looked at her. She reached out for some cookies and passed them on to Samantha. 'Take Nathan and go to your room.'

'I need to know what happened to Dad!' Samantha exclaimed. 'Who's downstairs?' She heard a man slightly groan.

'You deserve every detailed explanation. But for now, just look after Nathan and do not let him get out of that room.'

'This is not fair. I have the right to know where my father is!' Samantha yelled in a disappointing tone and slammed the door.

'You do,' Linette whispered to the door.

After taking a moment, Linette rushed toward Hunter to help him up. Looking into her worried eyes, Hunter frowned. 'Worrying after pushing me down—typical Linette.'

'My kids would've been—'

'Frightened. I know.'

In an intention to re-dress his wound, she settled him down on the couch and looked for medical tapes on the shelf. Her hands wandered as they failed to coordinate with her eyes.

Hunter held back a thought. Linette felt the tension in the air as she started giving him the medical care he needed.

'Samantha's mine, isn't she?' Hunter caught her lie.

Linette gulped and chose to ignore his words. Her eyes failed to believe her own lie. Another heartbreaking moment was about to conquer, and she wasn't ready for it.

'Why did you lie to me?' Hunter's voice broke. 'You said you were carrying Aaron's child.'

Linette inhaled sharply. 'Hunter, I am sorry.'

'You're sorry?!'

'After marriage, when I went for my first check-up with Aaron, they said my fetus was three months old and at that moment, we knew it was yours, not Aaron's. But we were already married!'

'I see Aaron didn't mind that. And you both kept my precious daughter, not giving a damn about telling me!' Hunter laughed; he was exhausted. 'I saw your lies right through you, as always. Allow me to show myself out.' Knowing Linette was already suffering from her husband's death, Hunter did not want to burden her.

Back at Gracy's place.

The doorbell rang.

On the other side, stood a goofy couple. For the world, they were Edgard and Abigail Ainsworth. Stepping into the real world was quite a task for them. They moved cities to cities, worked night shifts, did everything to give Eric a normal childhood—and were successful in doing so. The Aristarchus family had been in small businesses. Edgard used his Fenjiyawa blood to start one in Maryland.

What were the chances of them still carrying their true identities in the back of their mind? The island had a huge impact on them, but it 'wasn't worth remembering,' as Abiyeth says. Something on the other side of that door was going to remind them of their roots.

Eric received the impatient knocks to jolly faces.

'Eric!' the couple exclaimed.

'How was the journey?' Eric made way for them to enter.

'I had to apply for a permit to enter Annapolis, but I'm not complaining. Crazy virus, huh?' Emanuel replied.

Seeing the chaotic environment, Abiyeth stood near the staircase, uncomfortably. 'Everyone here looks busy, who are they?' The aura was too intense for her. The chattering of the people made her dizzy.

'We should go upstairs,' Eric said, impatiently, before Erica could get to them.

But it was too late. Erica's eyes had already found them in the midst of the chaotic crowd. She walked toward them and greeted them with a frown. Abiyeth smiled awkwardly, unaware of what Erica's expressions meant.

'Is it a little weird to say that you look like someone awful; awfully look like someone! Pardon my playful words.' Abiyeth scanned her appearance.

'Perhaps, you.' Ignoring the instructions given by Eric, she continued, 'Don't you remember the face of your daughter, who you left behind?'

'Unbelievable.' Eric whispered. 'Erica!'

'Right, my apologies, we haven't officially met. Erica Aristarchus—Abiyeth and Emanuel.'

'Let's take this upstairs.' Eric had no idea how much this had affected his parents.

The word "shock" is an understatement for what they felt. Running away from the island was a life-changing decision for them, if it weren't for the boat, they would've suffered on an island. It was as if Fenjiyawa was latched onto them. Erica did say, 'Once you enter the island, there's no going back.'

They struggled with words. Meeting up with their past lives—not in their itinerary.

Eric grabbed Erica's arm as she flinched. 'I told you to wait,' he hushed his voice.

'Try to look at it from my point of shoes.' She mixed up the phrases in confidence.

'That means nothing!'

Abiyeth was lost in old evocation. Eric saw his parents. They seemed traumatized. He gave the Fenjiyawa lass a severe look and took them to the bedroom.

Unconsciously, their legs made it to the bedroom. Eric sat on the corner of the bed, facing them, as they leaned against the headboard. They exchanged their silence and glances of disappointment.

'A bunch of researchers traveled to Fenjiyawa,' Eric broke the silence. 'Diseased people got them there. None of them, except for two, made it back. One of them was infected with the virus you developed.' He looked at his father. 'This is the virus outbreak everyone's panicking about. Quite unfortunate, right, father?'

'Eric!' Abiyeth interrupted.

'We cannot give this world another pandemic,' Emanuel whispered.

'Erica hopped into their ship while they were leaving. We have to go back to Fenjiyawa to get the vaccine.'

'No no no no no no no.' Shiver ran down Abiyeth's spine.

'Eric, you don't know what that island is,' Emanuel added. He had a flashback of some horrifying events. 'We can't go back there.'

Erica entered the room. All eyes were on her. Her eyes were on Abiyeth—her biological mother. She stared at her steadily. Looking for resemblance, she did find a few. Their eyes, their face structure, the way they tuck their hair behind their ears.

'I don't know what to say,' Abiyeth admired Erica. 'I see your father in you.'

'Or you could've asked how I've been.' Erica was crushed. The last thing she wanted to see in herself was her father.

'We know the answer to that,' Emanuel entered the conversation. 'Apologies won't cover the fact that you had a terrible childhood.'

'Then we'll need a substitute—going back to Fenjiyawa.'

At Linette's house.

'You can't leave the house until you recover,' Linette ordered. Her voice took a different tone—a tone Hunter was listening to after a long time, a tone he could never rebel against. 'You're staying.'

'Fine, keep me here against my will.' His eyes wandered for a while till they stopped at Gracy's house. 'What's the chaos about? Why is everyone at her place?'

'They're planning to go to Fenjiyawa to get the vaccine.'

'That's literally the entire team, just without me. I have to go.'

'You're not going anywhere with that fresh wound.'

'Watch me.'

'Hunter, no.'

'You don't own me!' He shouted and stomped his legs. He knew he had gone too far. Watching her eyes clench with fear, he looked down. 'I'm sorry. I'll stay.'

'I'll go get the meds.' Linette found an excuse to sulk upstairs.

Hunter groaned at the empty hall. He let out a few loud breaths and prepared himself for a lift. He held his breath and clenched the hand rest to pick himself up. Every time his body rose up an inch, he would heavily fall back. His biggest weakness was feeling weak. While the others hustled, he sat there. He preferred being an asset. A physical push didn't work for him, maybe a verbal push could do the work.

'Why are you still here?' asked a silvery voice from the upper floor.

Hunter frowned and turned his head toward the voice. 'Samantha?' He looked at her differently this time. Her green eyes—they were real. He was looking at his daughter.

'I know everything. I was listening.'

'You were? Look, don't blame your mother—'

'I see how you're trying to get close to my mother. Just because dad isn't around anymore, that doesn't mean she has no more feelings left for him. She still loves him, and you're getting in the way, outsider. I haven't even seen you before, who even are you?'

'Wait, what?'

'She doesn't understand it, but I do. She's vulnerable now, and you're taking huge advantage of that. It's best if you get away from us. Just leave!'

Hurt? Hunter was broken. Wasn't the hidden news already very devastating that the universe had to shove hurtful words in him, from his own daughter? He saw nothing but pure hate in those eyes—those beautiful green eyes. His body hit him with a certain agony. The physical wound was nothing in front of the mental one.

He clenched his teeth, holding the tears at the back of his eyes. 'You're right, I thought I had a chance,' his voice broke. 'I will leave.' Lying was an easy way out.

He got up, stronger this time, and left the house while Samantha watched. She was proud of her little speech, she thought she did something, saved her mother from an invader. She quietly went back to her room, smirking. No guilt.

Linette took a trip to the washroom to cleanse the dullness off her face, unaware of the painful conversation that happened in her absence. The cold water against her sorrow calmed her down. She then fetched the medicines and descended downstairs. The living room was empty. In search of Hunter, her eyes looked through the window. She found him limping toward Gracy's house. Linette sighed in despair and installed herself on the couch.

At Gracy's doorstep.

She received the door and waited for an explanation.

'Gracy, I feel fine.' Hunter went out of breath.

'You walked from Linette's to here and you're already exhausted.'

'It's sunny.'

'Officer Callahan, you are supposed to be resting.'
'Grace, count me in for the island.'

Chapter 13: Do You Believe Me?

She sat down in the corner of her kitchen, wondering how her life would have been if it were not for the atrocious activities happening around her. Everything was finally coming together for her. She felt as if she belonged to nothing. Her brain was tired of functioning more than anyone's caliber. She watched them quarrel. The chaos made her feel nauseous. Looking at Linette's door, however, she realized her problems were minimal in front of what that woman was going through.

She purposely kneaded her eyes till her vision got blurry. Those were a few seconds of not witnessing the pandemonium. Overlapping voices started penetrating through her ears, that is until Eric's soft voice took over.

'Grace?' He gently shook her till she could come back to her senses.

Her fatigue lips managed to construct a weak smile.

'Talk to me.'

'My brain hurts.' Words were eagerly waiting to come out. 'My eyes hurt. My hands are stiff. I am tired of pulling the trigger on innocent, innocent people! I'm a murderer.'

'Don't say that. You were brave enough to do what had to be done. You saved so many people by killing the infected ones. In the movies, they do it without shame.'

'Movies.' Gracy scoffed. 'Your parents here?'

'They're upstairs. This big mouth.' He watched Erica come down the stairs, 'Told them everything. You should go upstairs, meet them, tell them this plan is on regardless of what they feel.'

'We do need to get the vaccine.' Saying these words, she went upstairs to meet the Fenjiyawa folks.

Eric found an opportunity to confront his sister. Looking at her, his inner brother started coming into existence. He loathed the fact that he was turning her into his sister. Here we go again, he thought.

'What are you looking at me for?' Erica interrupted his thoughts, popping a wet cherry into her mouth.

'Did I not say I'll do the talking?'

'This cherry is tasteless, Fenjiyawa has better ones.'

'You little shit.'

'I was raised by Fenjees, you can't expect me to follow all the rules. Besides, this was rotting inside of me for years. You're the little shit, you're a big shit, biggest shit I've ever seen till date!'

Eric sighed and took her words into consideration. 'OK! OK, I'm sorry, you're right.' He then lowered his voice in an intention for Erica to hear it, yet kept it very subtle, 'Welcome to the family.'

Erica heard it loud and clear. With time, her feelings couldn't help it either. Staying with them made her feel that the real world wasn't quite as bad as she was told. Now, she did want to show compassion toward them, but a few things held her back in doing so. A few things she hadn't yet revealed.

Upstairs.

Abiyeth and Emanuel finally met Gracy. They got the insight they needed—how Erica made it to the real world and how the virus started spreading rapidly. They were still very reluctant about the idea of going to Fenjiyawa. After all, only they knew what the island did to innocent lives.

'After all these years, we're back at it again. This virus is following me.' Emanuel's body trembled with fear. 'Is Inhune still alive?' He adjusted his slipping specs as they smoothly slid against his nose.

'No, he's dead. The Fenjees are all on their own now. We need to get the vaccine.' Gracy's leg started shaking, her anxiety started acting up. Looking at Eric's parents, half-convinced, she put in more effort. 'We haven't alerted the health authorities yet, they're still not over the last pandemic. I don't wanna give them a second virus outbreak, especially not from Annapolis.'

'Well, tell them to go to Fenjiyawa and get the vaccine themselves.'

'They've already sent a ship there once, and look what that resulted into.'

Eric joined the conversation as he walked into the room with Erica. 'Why will they believe that the vaccine is somewhere in the middle of the ocean, on an island?'

'Because that's where it came from!' Emanuel yelled, done with everyone trying to manipulate him into agreeing. He laid back and sighed. 'Do they even know who the index patient is?'

'Aaron O'Malley, yes, they know. The president was the one who sent them there—it was confidential, and it still is. They're not revealing the source of the virus.'

Emanuel huffed and waited for a while. 'Abiyeth and I will come too.'

'The more the merrier!' Erica broke the calm environment.

Watching her agree to more people getting involved seemed fishy to Eric. How come she minded everyone else but the parents? It felt as if the agreement was loitering around her tongue, waiting for them to ask if they could join.

Being the most experienced people in the room, Abiyeth and Emanuel did not wait around for their son to agree. The married couple looked at each other and came to a final decision—they were definitely on board. Eric's convincing wouldn't influence their decision anymore. Knowing this, he didn't even try to talk them out of it.

'Alright,' Eric muttered, nodding his head as he watched them pull up their already packed bags.

The doorbell rang again. They were not expecting anyone else. Who could that be, Gracy thought to herself. Opening the door, tiredly this time, she found Linette on the other side. 'Are you alright?'

Linette wanted to say something but did not know how to. Her mind was bouncing between two replies—it was either 'just wanted to check up on you guys' or 'involve me in your plan.' She chose the latter. She went for the adventurous one. This was one of her most spontaneous decisions, another one being leaving Hunter for Aaron. 'Please take me with you guys,' Linette pleaded.

'I don't think that's a smart idea. What about your kids?'

'I can leave them at their aunt's. I need to do this, for exposure.'

Hunter overheard their conversation and felt the need to join in. 'Exposure for what? Stay with your kids, they need you.'

Ignoring his words, Linette continued, 'Aaron is dead because of that island. I need to be a part of this expedition. Maybe if I go there… Gracy, what would you do if it was Eric? Besides, you need a person who has medical experience, get all the help you can, right?'

Gracy raised her eyebrows and crossed her arms. 'I don't know why I am allowing you to do this. We do need medical help, just in case. You can tag along.' Not thinking twice is unlike her, a newly evolved Officer Brown was on the go.

Hunter walked away, still thinking it wasn't the best decision to let her in. In addition to that, they had to cram up in a ship together for days, and he wasn't ready for it. He heard faint voices, a conversation between Gracy and Roger.

'Did you speak to the captain?' Gracy asked.

Roger scoffed. 'You know what he said?'

'Please tell me he agreed.'

'Oh, he did. In fact, he's up for it tomorrow. Know why? He's going to ask you for a huge amount of money, oh and he wants to see me piss my pants on that island risking my life.'

Gracy, trying to hide her relief, cleared her throat. 'Don't worry about the money, we'll handle that part. The trip's tomorrow. Great.' She knew they weren't quite ready for an immediate trip, however, they had less time.

Roger shrugged his shoulders, showing no expressions, and walked away. Only he knew how much he feared the island, he wouldn't expect them to know his pain.

Hunter quietly stood in front of Gracy and questioned, 'Why are we allowing Mrs. O'Malley to "tag along?" She has no business being there.'

Gracy looked at his fresh wound and replied, 'Question is—why am I allowing *you*?'

'I am an officer.'

'A *wounded* officer. She's a *healthy* medic.' Gracy's eyes were still locked on his wound. Blood stains started spreading over his white cloth-like ink. It was getting worse.

'I feel fine,' he mumbled.

'You say that a lot.' Gracy shrugged her shoulders and walked away, imitating Roger's expressions.

Chapter 14: The More the Deadlier

Day one

The very next day, everyone left for the voyage. They headed toward the harbor and parked inside a shady lot. Everything happened under a dark shadow, this was yet another confidential trip to Fenjiyawa. They were loaded with ammunition and medical appliances. They were prepared, they presumed. Packing a map seemed unnecessary since Fenjiyawa was an unidentified island, yet they did carry one.

The captain had given them a specific location, a small brown shack, only a few meters away from the anchored ship. This isolated area gave them an advantage of making a deal with the captain, a deal they did not see coming. They stood beside the shack, their feet crunching on dry leaves, waiting for the man of the ship to arrive. Hearing the sound of the waves against the rocks, they could smell their destination—shit just got real.

A man, around forty years in age, came walking toward them. He wore his neatly pressed uniform and walked with an attitude as he firmly fixed his cap. A strong ship aroma started reaching their lungs as he approached them.

'Ahoy, me hearties! Bligh Thomas, your captain.' He put his hand forward, waiting for someone to take it.

'Hello.' Roger ignored the handshake and stood there in embarrassment.

'Thank you for doing this,' said Eric.

'Anything for my country, sire.' He stopped for a proud smolder. 'However, for the safety of my crew members, we will drop you off on the island and sail around in the open sea area till you shoot your flare and call us back. We, under no circumstances, will anchor our ship on that island—we've done that before and oh blimey, the horror! Since this is an illegal act, on being caught, me crew and I will be speaking against you.'

'He's overdoing the pirate language.' Marcos passed a comment to Zachery as they quietly scoffed.

'The story is simple! You all kidnapped our families and made us do it,' continued the captain as everyone stared at him disgustedly.

'What now?' Marcos raised his eyebrows. 'You're talking to a bunch of officers.' He stepped forward.

'I'm talking to a bunch of people who need me right now.' The captain's voice took a cocky tone.

'That seems dumb. I thought you said you'd do anything for your country.' Erica frowned in confusion.

'Sorry, miss, is there a problem?'

'If you really want to know my problem—'

'Erica.' Gracy sighed. 'We won't have any issues with you as long as you stop playing your little games and take us to the ship. We're paying you in amounts you probably never smelt before. Who needs who now?'

Bligh, feeling intimidated, announced loudly, 'Fantastic! Follow me.' He turned and walked toward the shore.

The walk wasn't a long one. The essence of the sea got stronger, they were walking with a certain stiffness in their hearts—a voice in their heads asking them to turn back. A few more steps further and they finally stood below the anchored ship. She was enormous, a heavy white ship, beautifully prepared for her mariners.

They had to go through a wide wooden plank, it was quite unstable and rather weird, to enter a majestic ship through a plank this unstable.

Once everyone boarded the ship, the crew members did not take time to release the anchor. They slowly sailed off and watched them get separated from their home land. At that very moment, everyone felt currents rushing through their veins.

The ship on the other hand—a true beauty. There were around ten rooms, one restaurant, one bar, and one conference room. She sailed on the water confidently, without hesitation.

Roger did not notice her beauty, rather he looked at the front desk and remembered a moment .

'I'm not saying he's stupid, but he does do the unnecessary pirate language,' said Aaron.

'And he has a wife?' William laughed.

'Beautiful like the moon,' Roger replied, raising his half-full glass against the full moon.

'I call that beauty with no brains to marry someone like Captain Bligh Thomas.' Scoffed Akshay, drunk.

'Watch it, she was my fiancé and he's my brother,' Roger said, not realizing his drunk voice was taking over.

Everyone bolted upright and spat out their drink at each other.

'How drunk are you?' William lowered his voice.

Roger looked at the startled faces and laughed in pain. 'I have secrets. At least I had 'em. What's my last name, men?'

Everyone was quiet, they looked at each other and raised their eyebrows.

'Exactly, no one knows. Hi, I'm Roger Thomas. Nice to meet y'all.'

'Bitch,' Ryan murmured. 'You never gave away your last name.'

'So that people don't know my family background. My parents aren't dead, I left the house because I hated the fact that they had an illegal drug dealing business on the run. They're still alive, I think. My elder brother, Bligh Thomas, left the house with me. We grew up together and he was pretty much supportive until I fell in love with this beautiful woman, Rosette. Bligh knew that. Months into my engagement with Rosette, I found my fiancé and my brother in bed—I walked in on them and I still remember their faces' Roger laughed, no one else did. 'Our paths often meet, we've seen each other a lot of times before but we behave as if we're strangers. We know each other—none of us are gonna start a conversation. The egoistic side of the Thomas brothers.'

'And you're OK with that?' Gale burped.

Roger shrugged his shoulders and drank directly from the bottle. After a long pause, he smirked and raised his alcohol. 'I earned this.'

Every moment passed by his eyes, he could feel their presence. Everyone had someone to go back to, Roger did not. He stood there in solitary, wishing for the island to take him instead of his friends—but it was too late. He looked at Bligh, they exchanged expressionless glances, and none of them looked away. In their eyes, the first one to look away would be a coward.

Bligh was rather proud of his brother for acting up. He agreed to this trip only for one reason—to get back his brother's trust. He meant well, all the fighting was no good and he was bored of their rivalry. He smirked and walked away, nodding his head, admiring Roger's stubbornness.

Roger took a deep breath and looked down, cursing the decisions that led him back to the island. He was a shuttle in between two rackets, in an endless game—his thoughts went from "why did I agree to do this" to "I can finally go back for some closure." He looked back at the empty space where Bligh was standing before. His thoughts were jumbled, he didn't realize that his brain was asking him to give Bligh another chance.

Inside the hallway of the ship.

Linette heard loud noises of retching. Slowly rushing toward the sound, she reached a door through which she heard muffled noises and pushed it inward. She stared right at Jacob, who held the rims of the lavatory and puked forcefully into it. 'I'm sorry,' she gasped and looked away. 'Sea sick?' She heard him breathe in intervals.

Jacob wiped his face and weakly rested his back against the wall. 'Received disturbing images of those zombies.'

'Zombies?' She scoffed.

'Lady, don't judge me, everyone's calling it.'

'Oh no, I was once a zombie fan.'

'Until your husband turned—' Jacob gulped. 'No offense.'

'None taken.'

'I owe you an apology. During the investigation, I spoke poorly to you. It was nothing personal, I just wanted to look cool—'

'In front of a woman you adore.'

'I didn't know it was that obvious.'

'It's not. Listen, kid, if you want to win someone over, don't be a jackass. Some people don't get blown away with rudeness, you need to be kind, and Poppy seems to be someone who would want an authoritative yet a delicate man.'

'So it *is* obvious.'

'Only she doesn't see it.'

They chuckled until Hunter limped by. His subtle eye roll was loud enough for Linette to acknowledge it. 'Take care,' she said to Jacob before catching up with Hunter, which seemed pretty easy.

'What brings you to this trip?' Hunter stopped mid hallway as he held his wound and looked at Linette.

'I told you, I want closure—'

'Bullshit. We both know why you left your children with your sister, who you hate, and decided to "tag along." Tell me you're not here to babysit me.'

'I am not here to babysit you.' She looked away.

'Come again, but I want you to look into my eyes and say it this time.'

Linette looked back at him but was silent.

'They never lie. Linette, I appreciate you looking after me but you are risking your life for no reason. You make spontaneous decisions and they are always bad. Your kids needed you there, for fuck's sake, I needed you there.'

'Why do we always end up talking about what I did years ago?'

'It's not easy for some people to get over an incident!' Hunter grunted and tightened his grip around the wound. He squeezed his eye as stress pinched his healing flesh. As the pain started decreasing, he slowly relaxed and let go of his wound. 'I need to go find some work.' Hunter started walking away.

'You need rest!'

'That's babysitting!' Hunter's voice echoed in the hallway as he disappeared out of the corridor.

Day two.

Gracy stood on the front deck with her binoculars, impatiently waiting for her eyes to get a glimpse of Fenjiyawa. She tapped on the binoculars and longed for at least a tiny dot.

'Come back tomorrow, maybe then you'll be able to feed your cravings.' Eric smiled.

'It seems sketchy.' She turned around and rested her shoulders on the wet railing. Through the glass doors, she watched Erica on the other side of the ship. 'I want to trust her, Eric. I really do, but something keeps pulling me back.'

'I know, it's difficult to trust someone who—'

'She adapted to the most impossible situation very easily. On the other hand, you had to go through self-therapy and a lot of convincing to trust the fact that she's your sister—that's a normal human reaction.'

'She is built differently. Look at her, look at where she was raised. The most impossible thing she had to adapt to was human beings eating each other on that island.'

Gracy relaxed her face and looked at Eric. 'You're right, it must have been hard for her.' After a moment of silence, she continued, 'I've been wondering, subtracting all the negative reasons why we are on this ship.' She removed a tiffany box from her handbag that was propped up against her leg. She opened the lid and revealed a beautiful platinum ring. 'I have a feeling this is the only alone time I'll get with you.' She watched him press his lips, not realizing how wide his smile had gotten. She took his hand and slipped the ring onto his finger.

Eric looked down and admired the ring. 'Why now?'

'Just in case things don't go our way on that island.' They looked at Erica, peacefully watching the ocean waves.

Erica found the perfect moment to re-think her plan. Behind the back of her brain, she kept playing memories of how Fenjees told her that people outside the island were the most horrible creations. But these people treat me as one of their own, she thought. Am I to give away the reason why I'm taking them to—

Her thoughts were left incomplete as Abiyeth and Emanuel entered her space. Abiyeth, keeping a light environment, offered Erica some cheese sandwiches. She took one and filled her mouth.

While watching her enjoy the meal, Abiyeth hesitantly started speaking. 'You ought to know, child, that we did send help thrice, to be accurate.'

'No one came back so we thought the sailors might have not survived the storm or the island,' Emanuel joined the conversation.

'We did not want to give up.'

'I had given my word to your father, we took a riskier path. I pulled a few strings together and managed to give an anonymous tip to the officials.'

'We twisted the story a little. We told them that there is land, owned by no one, where they can develop and hide their nuclear weapon—assuming they needed one. I gave all the evidence of the existence of that island and they believed it. And then—'

'And then the President came to us,' Roger added as he walked toward them. 'And we went to the island completely unaware of what it had become.'

'You're one of them?'

'There is no *them*.' Rogers' body shivered as he kept his hands warm inside the pockets of his jacket. He was filled with rage but he was exhausted to show it—exhausted with all the worrying, exhausted with reliving those moments, exhausted after what life had taken away from him. He had no voice to raise. He looked at Emanuel, wishing he could let out a punch, however, he scoffed and walked away as he lit a cigarette. They died for no reason, he thought.

Erica had zoned out. She was drowning in her own thoughts until Emanuel called out her name and her eyes flickered as she came back to her senses. 'I might have something to confess,' she whispered.

'What is it, dear?' Abiyeth asked in concern.

'I—these sandwiches are really tasty. Can I get some more?'

'Why not, honey! We'll make more for you.' Abiyeth smiled and she looked at Emanuel. They both walked toward the kitchen, not noticing her call for help.

Erica turned toward the waves and kept her hands on the railing as she hyperventilated. She closed her eye lids tightly and started whispering sentences that she was told. 'They are not family. They left us. They left us here to die,' she repeated unless it got registered back into her mischievous brain. Her final decision—once I open both my eyes, I will not fall for their kindness. Sticking to her decision, she opened her eyes and smirked at the empty, dead-calm ocean.

Day three.

They noticed a small dot of land located far away. Gracy was relieved yet horrified to see it.

'How come there's no mark of Fenjiyawa on any of these maps?' asked Poppy as she filled her hands with three different detailed maps.

'You mark only what you discover, and once people entered Fenjiyawa, there was no going back and putting a name on it.' Erica smiled proudly.

'Yep, definitely looking forward to entering this island,' Maverick prompted sarcastically.

'All we know is that it's in the denser parts of the Pacific Ocean,' Gracy murmured as she tried to look through the binoculars.

'We have a clipper!' exclaimed the captain, unnecessarily.

'A what?' asked Eric.

'A fast-moving ship, sire. She's one hell of a ship I must say.'

'She sure is,' Linette added.

'By the way, Officer Brown, they found Sophia. There's no proper range here but all they said was that they found her. She's safe, OK? No more blaming me for something I didn't do,' Jacob announced.

'We're all dead anyway.' Bligh's tone changed as everyone raised their eyebrows.

'That's not very pleasant.' Linette was concerned as she watched Bligh walk away, toward Roger—on the far end of the ship.

'Is this how you're going to repay me? With silence? You owe me an adult conversation.' Bligh walked toward Roger as he watched his brother resting his hand on the railing, quietly watching the waves, keeping his sight away from Fenjiyawa.

'Why do you think I owe you anything, Bligh?' Roger kept his vision fixed on the surface of the groovy water.

'I was a weak man drawn toward a beautiful lady. I wasn't much of a charmer back then. The only woman to ever look at me was she, and I fell for those eyes.'

'Not much of an apology, Bligh.' Roger turned toward Bligh.

'I'm not trying to apologize; I'm trying to reason with you.'

'What do you know about reasoning?' Roger looked into his proud eyes. 'Talk to me when you have regret in those perverted eyes of yours.'

'Why do you think I would ever regret my decision?'

'Because you lost a brother.'

'Gained a family instead.'

'My family.' Roger's face did not twitch an inch. 'Talk to me when you have regret in your eyes.' He repeated and walked away.

Bligh Thomas scoffed to himself.

'You know why I don't have any regrets, Darla?' He spoke to his ship. 'Because I saved him from a cheater, I wasn't the only man she slept with—oh Rosette, red lips, soft hair, beautifully maintained body, smelt of roses.' He closed his eyes and imagined her smile. Bligh wanted Roger to think he had a family with Rosette, but little did Roger know that Bligh left her the moment they were caught. 'I wanted him to walk in on us. She was wrong for my little brother.'

Day four.

'How about a shot of love for everyone?' Erica announced and passed on an unusual drink in tiny glasses. It tasted of bourbon with a hint of orange. 'I figured you people drink before any risky task—I'd never know why.'

'Gives us a kick I guess, thank you.' Jacob grabbed one glass and gulped it down his throat at once.

Erica offered some to Linette. 'I don't drink.' She refused with a smile.

'Good luck getting bourbon down her throat.' Hunter scoffed.

Offended, Linette stared at the glass for a whole minute before chugging it down, proving Hunter wrong—it seemed important for her to rebel against his every word. She looked at him with stern eyes as he looked away with disappointment. He knew she was turning into someone he would never be able to handle.

Moments passed by.

The ship was finally at the foot of Fenjiyawa, caressing its sand. They were asked to climb down while it floated, not even anchored. The crew members threw down, yet again, an unstable ladder. A beautiful ship but the ways to get in and out of it, not so commendable.

Everyone climbed down, one by one.

The captain handed Erica a flare gun. 'Shoot this up in the air and we will be there!'

'I'm rather tempted to shoot this up to your—'

'Erica!' Eric called her from below the ship.

'Feisty little woman!' exclaimed the captain as he laughed nervously.

Everyone, except the captain and the crew members, stepped on the island. Eyes were wide open, ears were awake and bodies were ready to fight danger.

'It's quiet,' Eric said in a soft voice.

'No, everything is muffled.' Jacob vigorously rubbed his ears.

'Emanuel, dear, I'm not feeling quite well.' Abiyeth's head felt heavier than usual.

'Strange, me neither.' Gracy's surroundings got indistinct. She looked at her hands and then moved her blurry vision toward Eric who had already fallen to the ground.

Erica watched Gracy lose her consciousness and faint against the ground. 'I haven't been truthful to any of you.'

Chapter 15: I Am Back, Brother

Pain—oh what a thing to experience. Physical or mental—which pain would you choose? Hint: Physical pain heals over time.

They opened their eyes to gray clouds and strong winds. Their eyeballs tried to adjust themselves after a long, painful rest. Blue-sky spirits were the first thing they saw as they squeezed their eyelids to make it go away. Finally coming into their senses, they found their bodies, legs, and hands tied against the trunk of the trees, with thick jute ropes. Everyone groaned as they started feeling a certain tightness in their facial muscles. They felt a faint metallic taste in their mouth. They felt weaker than usual. Fear had taken place in the domain.

Hunter was already in so much pain—he couldn't struggle to get out.

Linette stood there, focusing on her breath as her eyes were in search of Hunter.

Roger's body shivered as it went cold blue.

Emanuel and Abiyeth were the only ones to be tied up against the same tree. They held each other's hands and stayed calm.

Jacob and Zachery tried pushing themselves forward to loosen the rope but it was as tight as a bow string.

Poppy, Maverick, and Hendricks were dizzy and still hadn't realized their state.

Marcos and Alexis panted in dread.

Gracy felt betrayed and had no vitality left in her.

Eric tried moving his head around, in search of everyone. He shrieked in anger after noticing that they were all tied up against alternative trees. He squirmed to escape from the triple-knotted rope. His face turned red and his arms purple, but the rope was intact. He stomped his leg in vexation.

'Gracy!' He called out, with all the strength he had left in him.

'I'm right here!' she yelled back, feebly.

He was relieved that her voice was somewhere near him. He, again, tried turning his head toward the voice but unfortunately, the rope was intact.

After everyone called out each other's names, they realized one was missing.

'She tricked us!' Jacob cried out loud as he tried to force himself out of the rope.

'She did not!' Eric defended, trying to reach the knot with his trembling hands. Upon the realization of his empty ring finger, he cried silently.

No one could get out of this trap. All their weapons were taken away. This seemed like a plan that was brewing for years.

'I bet it's that drink she gave us!' Marcos cried out loud, tasting numbness on his tongue. 'Everyone's here except for—'

'Erica Aristarchus,' announced a grating voice from behind.

A tall man in his fifties walked toward them. He carried a polished copper stick that pushed his legs forward on the dry, rocky land. His face was wrinkled with rage and revenge. His hair had turned gray over the years of betrayal.

'Inhune?' Emanuel recognized the ruthless voice. It had been years since he had heard pure hate in someone's voice.

'What is happening?' Linette cried, the poor clueless thing still struggling to get out.

They heard crunching noises of footsteps against the dried-up leaves. Inhune walked by every tied body, looking at their faces, enjoying the sight of them pleading to set them free. He laughed and stopped in front of Emanuel, his stick in front of him as he rested both his hands on the tip of the copper. He looked at his brother and yelled, 'Good job, lass!' No doubt it was directed to Erica, acknowledging her brave work of managing to get everyone back to the island.

'What is this?' Abiyeth whispered loud enough for Inhune to hear it.

'Please darling, I will answer all your questions. But first, let me reunite with my faithful brother.' Inhune's voice picked up a furious tone.

He firmly held Emanuel's shoulder and scanned his body from head to toe, with a smirk. He held him so tightly that a red handprint was left behind. He clenched his teeth and recalled a few old words that were told by Emanuel.

'I will come back brother, you said. You have my word brother, *you* said!' Emanuel bawled as a powerful punch was thrown across his face.

He coughed out blood and wheezed in pain. He looked at Inhune through his partially closed eyes. He had no defense.

'No, Dad!' Eric shouted as he heard his father in distress.

'Oh, Dad?' Inhune looked at Eric and walked toward him. 'I've longed for this day.'

'Don't you dare touch my kid!' Abiyeth cried. He ignored her words.

He stood in front of Eric and let silence take over as they exchanged a furious look. 'Erica, look how weak your brother is, just like his father.' Inhune broke the stare.

Erica did not let her shiver show. Her mind could not construct sentences and words could not seem to be uttered. She watched Eric becoming weaker, her emotions were fighting to come out.

Inhune was astounded to hear her stillness. His smile wore off as he looked at her and grabbed a handful of her hair. 'Are you not enjoying this?'

Erica whimpered as she forcefully said, 'I am.' He smiled and let go of her. 'Weak, just like his father.'

'Eric Aristarchus!' Inhune announced. He felt Eric's anger the moment he tightly gripped his cheeks.

'The fight is with me, leave my son out of this!' Emanuel shouted in pain.

Inhune relaxed his hands and dusted off Eric's shirt.

Eric noticed his ring on Inhune's fingers; it barely fit him, yet he wore it proudly. 'How dare you!' Eric yelled as he tried running against the rope.

Inhune raised his eyebrows while watching him try his best to reach out. He lifted his stick and slammed it against Eric's leg, with great potency, almost breaking his shin. Dropping his stick, he prepared a fist and threw a punch across his face.

Eric panted as blood dripped from his busted lip. He groaned in intense pain but did not lower his gaze. 'Just give us the vaccine and let us go.' His words came out feebly.

'You hear that, lass?' Inhune laughed, but the lass was quiet.

Inhune's fury increased. He dreamt about enjoying this moment with his daughter but her emotions were interfering, which he clearly had erased. He rested his arms and looked at Erica. 'Enjoy with me, you filthy little creature!'

Erica mentally broke down, something she had never felt before. The real world had shown her a soft side, successfully eliminating the tough in her. As she was the bridge between the outside world and Fenjiyawa, Inhune kept her happy whenever he felt she was drifting away. He knew she craved his respect and took plenty of advantage. She did what she was told to do, Inhune was ready to show her the respect she deserves, then why was she not cherishing the moment?

'There is no vaccine.' Inhune directed Erica to hand him the fallen stick, and so she did. She herself did not understand why she was respecting her father's orders.

'What?' Eric looked at Erica, shocked. His eyes flickered, his mind wandered, and the trip to Fenjiyawa made no sense anymore. Erica did not look back at him, she couldn't.

Inhune walked toward Abiyeth and chuckled joyfully. 'My Abiyeth!' He gently caressed her face with his fingers. She looked back at him, disgustedly.

'Brother, please let them go.' Emanuel's voice took a low, respectful tone—that's how Inhune liked it.

'Brother?' Inhune sighed and immediately marched back to Emanuel. 'Brothers do not leave their own brothers to rot on an island filled with diseased beings! Do they?' On getting no reply from Emanuel, he whispered sinisterly, 'You are not my brother.'

'I wasn't thinking straight—'

'And now *I* am not thinking straight.' He turned back and announced loudly, 'Let's call out the Fenjees now, shall we?' He convoked a bunch of reckless human beings.

Around thirty Fenjees came forward, marching on the dry land with sharp wooden spears almost their height. They could be described as poorly dressed men and women—torn clothes, worn-out pants, no sign of hygiene.

Two of the Fenjees dragged a diseased man with them—of course he was trapped in a cage, waiting for his teeth to tear fresh meat.

The man had been infected for a long time, due to which he had enormous bumps all over his body. From the bump, oozed out a thick sticky yellow liquid. His spine was protruding out its back like a reptilian. He had no lips, only a full set of rotten teeth. He barely had any hair attached to his scalp. His jaw hung out as rotten blood drizzled out of it. His fingers were impatient and his flesh was loosely held by his bone. He was lifeless, yet in motion. He reached out his arms from the cage, trying to grab a source of nutrition.

'Mister Ansley is hungry!' Inhune smirked. 'I detest the fact that he's struggling to get food. You see, I owe him a little, he was a kind one. Alright! Let's pick a meal for him.' He walked past scared faces against the tree and stopped when he saw a calm one. 'You,' he declared. 'What's your name?'

'Linette,' she said in a low voice.

'Louder!' He craned his neck toward Linette.

'Linette!' she cried as her body shivered with fear.

Hunter gasped and agonized, 'I'll kill you if you touch her!'

Inhune laughed. 'We have a lover!' The Fenjees joined his laughter.

He sauntered toward Hunter and admired his gunshot wound. He looked at his beaten-up face with fake pity and clicked his tongue. 'Poor thing, you will kill me? Can you even stand straight?' Inhune turned around to walk away.

'Fuck you,' Hunter whispered. One thing Hunter could not handle was getting belittled by someone.

Inhune stopped. 'What did you say?' He still had his back on Hunter.

'Sooner or later, I will kill you!' said Hunter, loudly.

Inhune's wrinkled face twitched with anger. He raised his stick and jabbed it right through Hunter's wound. He did not even have to look at him. He was confident in his aim. He applied pressure to the stick and let it stay there for a couple of seconds as he twisted and made his way into his flesh. Hunter bellowed at the top of his voice. He clenched his teeth and panted as his saliva dripped uncontrollably. He had never felt that extreme pain before. The entire island echoed with his screams. After a long time, tears rolled down his cheeks. Sticky mucus rushed out his nose as he kept shrieking in pain. His veins were popping out, almost about to burst. He coughed out a blob of blood as he shivered. However, Hunter stood up straight and focused on his breathing.

Inhune rested his stick back on the ground as blood leaked from the rear tip. He walked away as if nothing had happened, stood in front of the Fenjees, beside Erica, and stated out loud, 'Get them out!' The Fenjees yanked Bligh Thomas and his crew members into the scene.

'Please stop! Let us go! We have nothing to do with this!' Bligh cried out loud.

'Bligh!' Roger yelled, knowing he was about to lose another family member.

'Inhune, let them go!' Emanuel pleaded.

Inhune leaned toward Bligh and whispered in his ears, 'Mister Ansley will have you today.' He drew himself back and watched the show.

This was the cue for Fenjees to shove Bligh Thomas inside the cage with infected Mister Ansley—a show to watch Bligh try to survive. He had no advantage, his hand and legs were tied. 'Roger!' He went for his last words. 'Rosette was a cheater! She was sleeping with ten other men!' Bligh's low voice took over the land, 'I knew your weak ass would've forgiven her after those men but not after me. I couldn't have you go run back to her. Now that I think of it, that whole drama was uncalled for, it was not worth losing my brother. I've always cared for you, Roger.'

Roger wanted to reply, he wanted his brother to hear his voice, but he was stiff. How did he manage to lose all those important people on the same island—he had nothing to say. His ears went numb, refusing to hear his brother's death.

'Weak.' Inhune showed no mercy. 'Brothers like you should be tortured.' He opened the cage and watched the Fenjees forcefully push Bligh inside as he tried wrestling. He stopped when he knew his life was coming to an end. He clenched his eyes and cried out loud as Mister Ansley started tearing off his neck.

Everyone yelled and struggled in unison. Erica looked away—Inhune hadn't filled her in on his evil plan. She felt responsible for what was about to come.

Slowly, the screams had stopped, Bligh Thomas was dead. Mister Ansley was taken away. Bligh was still in the cage, about to turn into one of their kind.

The screams were still alive in Roger's memory. He silently cried his brains out. He could not breathe in intervals. He was in shock.

Inhune, without wasting any time, gestured to the Fenjees to take one crew member each and stand in front of those who were tied against the trees. 'All of you are going to watch death! My Fenjees are going to perform and no one will miss the show.'

The crew members were outnumbered, there was no point in rebelling. They cried, they were helpless, and they had no clue why they were put in that position.

The Fenjees made them kneel down in front of the tied ones. In unison, they all raised their weapons and waited for Inhune's signal.

'Please don't do this to them,' Gracy pleaded. She was restless, she felt useless. More Fenjees came forth. They were ordered to rest a shiv on the necks of the watchers. 'If any of you look away, they will not hesitate to slit your throats. There will be no exceptions, so please watch our little performance.'

The crew members looked down, accepting defeat, still unaware of why they were dragged into that situation—they will never know.

Abiyeth cried out loud, 'Inhune please don't—'

Inhune commanded, 'Now!'

The spears went straight through the skulls of the crew members. Everyone screamed, cried out loud while the Fenjees laughed at their wretched state.

Erica was quiet, devastated.

After hearing the skull shatter, Poppy threw up with force. She was made to watch a sharp spear pierce through a man's brain with an eyeball stuck to the tip and blood all over her body. She was bound to gag at the flesh that came out.

'King Inhune! He looked away!' yelled one of the happy Fenjees.

'Oh c'mon! I told you not to look away or your throat will be slit! Cut him, my rules apply to everyone,' Inhune ordered.

'No, please don't!' Eric begged.

A hand was put against the muffled screaming, no last words were allowed to be delivered. The sharply polished shiv cut smoothly through the neck as the body seized.

'No!' Gracy squalled. 'Eric?!' She got no reply.

'Eric!' Abiyeth and Emanuel wailed in unison.

'Maverick!!!' Eric cried. He barely watched a Fenjee cut the rope that held Maverick against the tree as his body dropped to the ground. 'Maverick, you weak fuck! You never look away! Inhune, why are you doing this?!'

Eric could hear his own heartbeat. First, it was the only person who he truly looked up to and now his buddy. Universe took away important people from his life too. He watched Maverick's blood drip down on dead, dry leaves. His brain was shutting down. Watching two murders in less than a minute—not easy.

'Mave!' Hendricks cried out loud. 'What is wrong with you people?' Hendricks yelled.

'Shut him up.' Inhune's voice was as casual as it could have been.

Another shiv ran across a throat. Hendricks gurgled his blood as he tried to scream. Three murders in less than a minute. Eric blamed himself. He stood there, lifeless. 'Please, stop.' He cried.

Everyone was muted. Inhune was winning.

'The wait is over!' Inhune announced out loud while strolling by terror-stricken faces. 'So many questions, so many answers. How did all of you end up here? Simple. It was planned. Do you think Erica running into Eric was a coincidence? Innocent, innocent, dumb souls! I have been planning this since the day you left us. My whole life had been leading up to this very moment. The moment where I ruin each of your lives. I don't know most of you. I don't understand why you are here but—the more the merrier!

I started training Erica the second she turned ten. We gathered a lot of information about Abiyeth, Emanuel, Eric, and his beloved Gracy. You see, if we created a virus this harmful, we can create anything. It wasn't easy to find your location, but the vengeance in me made it easier.

After fishing you and your information out, we planned to get a ship here. Now comes the amusing part—Abiyeth and Emanuel, you told my lass you sent us that ship? My poor Erica believed it. When she told me this I was impressed. I waited until now to tell her that they were just playing, they wanted to make my lass feel sorry for them. They never sent us that ship, they never cared about us.

Eric Aristarchus, your parents are not as gullible as they seem. They are selfish! I contacted the President from this island, I gave them the location, I told him we have land for nuclear weapons—I know how to lure another king into a kingdom.

Once they made their way here, we purposely released the diseased beings on them. Erica made her way to the ship, as planned. You know the story after that.'

'If you are so intelligent, Inhune, why didn't you use this to save yourselves out of this island?' Emanuel scoffed with pain.

'Revenge over safety, brother—that's how an Aristarchus is wired. I can't be brutal out of this island, they have laws I've heard. Here, I make my own rules. Here, I make you suffer.'

Chapter 16: Outbreak

Zombie apocalypse. Why is it that every time there's a virus outbreak, people assume it's going to end up as a Zombie apocalypse? Simmer down, that's not science.

Marburg is the most dangerous virus with a fatality rate of up to 85%.

The viruses are known to be existential only after entering a healthy host. After the host is dead, the virus starts fading away in a few hours or sometimes, in a few months.

Zermaitus doesn't die in a dead host, it develops. The virus starts getting aggressive. With all the homo sapiens the virus captured, in less than two weeks, it officially became the most dangerous virus with a fatality rate of 100%. The risk of contamination was high, clearly.

Dr. Campbell had two dead bodies lying on the tables next to each other. Aaron's body and the body of Mr. Ted Rimes, who had died of an unknown cause. His organs were outside his body—ready to be examined. His head was cut open and a brain bulged out.

Raghav compared Ted's blood to Aaron's. They did not match. In fact, the body did not possess any signs of Zermaitus. He tested his blood, hoping for it to be the virus but the results were negative. His blood was normal. Then why was the body even sent to him?

Raghav was being ignorant, he was blinded by the plague happening around him. In this chaos, he did not feel the need to run small tests. He stared at the body, creating a therapy session with his inner-self. *Don't go too hard on yourself, you'll find the cure. You'll just have to dig deeper into this virus, he thought.*

A small syringe mark caught his eyes. He sighed in disappointment and rushed upstairs to dial the police officer number who had sent him the body.

'Greetings, officer. Where are you?' Raghav was calm.

'I'm at Ted Rimes' house,' replied the officer.

'Agent James Arthur, may I know why you have sent me this body?'

'You needed another specimen to examine. His wife mentioned all the symptoms you were looking for so I guessed he had the virus. Please don't call to thank me, I—'

'Your ignorance made me ignorant. Look around, do you see a syringe?'

After a pause, James did find a syringe fallen under the bed. 'Yeah, so?'

'He injected an empty syringe into his Carotid Artery. I know you love staying at the top of your game but do not compete with anyone in this situation—do your job right.' Dr. Campbell ended the call.

He started marching down to his morgue, murmuring to the stairs till he heard his wife come out of the room.

Elora Campbell. Ten years younger than her husband. She was Raghav's second wife after his first wife met with an unfortunate accident. They had two children, a 16-year-old stud—Noah, and a 12-year-old doll—Arabella.

'You're there all the time,' Elora said in the lowest voice possible, glancing at the clock. 'It's late.'

'Elora, the whole city is counting on me and my best investigators have disappeared. I need to find a vaccine soon and for that I need to know more about the virus.'

'But—'

'Sh,' he interrupted as he heard a low thump from his morgue. 'Did you hear that?'

'Yeah, it sounded like a man shushing his wife.' She crossed her arms.

He slowly climbed down the stairs as the noise started getting clearer. He entered the six-digit code to reveal the source of the clamor. To his shock, he saw an old man standing in front of him, showing his back. Raghav gasped and stepped back in horror. There was no other way for anyone to enter his morgue, so who was the man who managed to get into his private space?

The noise produced by opening the door caught the man's attention. He turned slowly, giving a head start for Raghav to run upstairs. However, his hurrying feet slipped as his head hit the step. The fall resulted in a minor concussion, enough for him to still stand back on his feet, in pain.

He whimpered. His eyes looked downstairs, in search of the man and there he was limping upstairs, preparing his appetite to be filled with human flesh.

Elora walked toward the chaos and saw Raghav's scared eyes. She followed his vision and was traumatized to see a pale man with his guts out.

The man was empty, he had no organs. His wrinkled body, weak bones, limbs barely attached to his body, and thick blood dropping off from whatever was left, terrified the couple.

'Raghav!' she cried, not knowing why he wasn't retrieving.

Raghav wasn't in shock, he was recalling a few unnecessary facts as he removed a scalpel from his pocket and stood up in valor. Stab their brains to end them, he thought as he started unboxing the thoughts he once felt were useless.

The man was one step away to get to his meal. Raghav gripped his scalpel tightly and gathered the courage to commit a crime.

The man growled at him before making a move. 'I'm sorry Mr. Ted Rimes, here goes nothing,' said Raghav as he held the man's collar and pierced the scalpel into his brain. He watched him drop dead on the ground as his body rolled back downstairs. Raghav did not gag. At once, he upgraded all his views about Zombies. All his walls of scientific knowledge broke down when a dead man came back to life.

He looked at Elora's petrified face and hissed. 'Make sure the children don't see this.'

At Evelyn's.

Samantha was furious. Their mother had left them in a horrifying situation, in a place where the population was decreasing. Linette had been taking wrong decisions her entire life, what was the harm in taking yet another erroneous decision?

The kids were quarantined in a house with their Aunt Evelyn, who detested them. Samantha always pictured her coming out of a doll factory. Evelyn McCarthy was unmarried. She never liked the idea of love, for her it was just a double-trouble game, bouncing from one man to another. She worked as a gym trainer—a 36-year-old woman happily trapped in a 20-year-old body.

Hunger brought Samantha and Nathan to march downstairs.

'We're hungry!' Samantha announced.

Evelyn sighed and asked, 'What do you want?'

'Pizza!' Nathan exclaimed.

'No, you can't have pizza.'

'Burger then.' Samantha smiled in sarcasm.

'I'm heating up some oat porridge for the both of you,' Evelyn replied with a dull face. She did not seem to enjoy their company. She was never a person who could force happiness on her face. If she hated anything, she would make sure to express it in every possible way.

'We'd rather starve to death,' Samantha groaned.

'Fine by me.'

A doorbell interrupted their platonic conversation. Evelyn groused and went toward the door. She was surprised when she looked through the peephole. It was one of her affairs. She asked the children to go upstairs and took a while to open the door as she started recalling his name.

'John!' she exclaimed as she opened the door.

'It's Harry.'

'Right! The city is under lockdown, so you should go—'

'You said you were gonna call.' Harry barged in.

Evelyn chuckled nervously, 'That doesn't sound like me.'

'You played with my emotions.' He walked toward her aggressively.

'Henry, I would never—'

'It's Harry!' He pushed her with great force. She saw his pupil disappearing while she picked herself up. He growled with wrath as fear appeared in her eyes.

Evelyn reached out to his shoulders to push him out of her house; however, he held her hand while piercing into her flesh with his blunt nails. He pulled her close and bit off a chunk of flesh from her neck. She shrieked in pain and with all her strength, she managed to kick him out of the house. She locked the door in shock and heard him bang the door for a good minute.

'That was new.' Aghast at his behavior, she ran upstairs as blood dripped on every step of the staircase. She opened the door open to find Samantha lazily scrolling through her phone, jamming into her earphones.

She rushed toward the cabinet and searched for a first aid kit. Her hasty moves caught Samantha's attention. She frowned and removed her earphones to unravel the cause of her abnormal behavior.

'What's with the panicking?' she pried.

Evelyn found a first aid kit as she pulled out a drawer. She turned around and rested it on the dressing table. Samantha noticed the bite and had mixed feelings about the situation. She was rather surprised to see her wish getting granted so expeditiously. She raised her eyebrows and moved forward to get a closer look, still keeping a safe distance between them.

She watched Evelyn's shaky hands unroll the bandage wrap as she took a long breath, preparing herself for an agonizing pain when she opened the rubbing alcohol bottle. She emptied half of the alcohol and screamed in pain.

'This hurts like a bitch!' Evelyn stomped her legs in pain as she started wrapping bandages around her wound.

'You really gotta watch your language around Nathan.' Samantha frowned.

'I don't see him around.'

'Well, he's in the washroom.'

'Then shut the hell up.'

Samantha nodded her head and calmly watched the scene. Evelyn fastened the wrap with a pin and looked into the mirror, resting her hands on the dressing table, trying to recall the horrendous incident.

'What in the name of hickey?' she murmured.

'How does my mom trust you with us?'

'She shouldn't.'

'Right. So what was that?'

'A man bit me.'

'He what?' Samantha let out a giggle.

Evelyn gave her a stare through the mirror.

'Sorry.' Samantha's voice wandered. 'What if—'

'No.'

'You didn't even let me complete my question.'

'If you're going to turn this scene into one of your zombie movies then I do not want to hear it, Samantha.'

'Well, it makes sense!'

Evelyn turned toward Samantha and assured her. 'Zombies do not exist.'

Samantha shrugged her shoulders. 'Where's Mom?'

'She didn't tell you? She's on an island, saving the world apparently.' Evelyn exited the room as she rolled her eyes.

'Saving the world. Does she think I'm four?' Samantha ranted to the empty room.

Nathan came out sobbing, looking for some comfort. 'Where Mommy?'

'Mommy's,' Samantha smiled, 'in a faraway land, saving the world.'

Raghav' s shivery hands started dragging the body back to his morgue. The beautifully flourished stairs had blood trails on them and Elora was not happy about it. He dropped the body's legs in order to focus on his breathing, trying to process the incident.

Elora stood there, stationary. The sight of her husband dragging a dead body into the house was quite eerie.

'El, help me out with this,' said Raghav as he lifted up the body's legs again.

'Like you ever helped me out with the dishes.' A panic statement.

Raghav raised his eyebrows at her reply. 'Are you comparing dishes to a dead body?'

'Why is it heavy anyway? You've removed all his organs, should be lighter than any of us.' She blurted out, without thinking.

'He is not heavy. My mind is heavy! My anxiety is not letting me focus on my strength. I am confused. There was no sign of the virus in his body! He was walking without a heart! His heart is chilling in my lab with his other organs, and he was here! He was walking! A zombie? It's not science!' He panicked too. He felt as if science had betrayed him. He wasn't quite wrong to feel that way, this really was absurd.

Elora chose silence. She had never seen him lose his mind in any situation and surely never heard him use the word "zombie" before. She quietly walked toward him and picked up the body's arms. Her hands were rather too skinny to hold bloated arms; however, she was determined.

Together, they lifted up the pale body and successfully dragged it to the morgue. Elora almost choked on her own vomit as she smelt the pungent environment. It was an extremely repellent part of their house.

'Let's make sense out of this,' Raghav continued. 'There were two bodies in the morgue. I kept the diseased brain beside a comparatively healthy, untouched brain. The virus was already active. It doesn't require an alive body to infect. It just needs to get inside a preserved brain.'

'But it wasn't preserved, he was dead.'

'It's beyond science. This virus is impressively advanced, it's intelligent. Its growth is inevitable. This body was fully exposed, so the virus found an opening and controlled its brain because evidently, that's where all our functions are stimulated. I'm impressed with my immunity, I have been in close contact with this virus for hours now.'

He looked at Elora's bare hands covered in thick blood. He then noticed his hands were protected with gloves, unlike hers.

'Don't be alarmed, but you need to go and take a good shower with the special disinfectant I keep behind the mirror. I'll meet you downstairs for a blood test.'

Without questioning, Elora sprinted upstairs, keeping her hands to herself. She stepped under the cold shower, her clothes still on, hyperventilating. Her bloody hands trembled but bit by bit, the stains bid adieu. She vigorously scrubbed herself and started undressing with her eyes tightly shut. She took a moment to breathe as she watched the mixture of blood and water go down the drain.

Downstairs, Raghav stood dead still in front of the two bodies. His pupils started constricting as he stared at them. He tried expanding his knowledge about viruses. He realized they were dealing with something more than that and did not know where to begin.

At Evelyn's house.

Samantha and Nathan had been stuck in their room for long enough. The water reached way above their heads; staying silent was not an option. 'I'll go get something to eat,' she whispered to Nathan. Having a pretty strong feeling about her aunt being infected, she decided to switch on her stealth mode.

She tiptoed downstairs as her hand caressed the dusty railing. The living room was empty. Her eyes were wide open, her ears were attentive and her hands were steady.

She walked toward the kitchen, her right hand carefully revealing what the refrigerator contained. She nodded when she found a pizza box lying inside, deliciously. An eight-piece, cold Margherita. She placed it on the platform and prompted, 'Bitch.'

'Sorry?' asked an angry voice from behind.

A shiver ran down Samantha's spine. Zombies couldn't talk, so she guessed they were still safe. The scared soul could not face the angry one. Without looking at her aunt, her legs worked their way up the stairs. A small glimpse, of Evelyn biting into the cold pizza, is all Samantha could get.

Disgusting, Samantha thought to herself. She went back to the room, empty-handed. Her mother's phone was unreachable. She was trapped in blood-curdling thoughts. Her eyes moved toward Nathan, who played with his toys, peacefully. He was unaware of the things happening around him. How Samantha wished she could trade places with him.

An hour passed by, and their hunger had increased. Samantha made a decision to flee away. She packed her backpack with a few essentials and handed Nathan a stuffed toy. 'For the love of God, do not cry.'

Their hungry feet managed to take them down the stairs. Samantha could feel her stomach growling, Nathan just felt like he could take a good nap in that silent surrounding.

Asking him to stay put by the door, Samantha walked toward the pizza box, cautiously. As she managed to grab it and firmly grip the cardboard, Evelyn showed up yet again. This time, her eyes were blood-shot, her body was pale yellow and veins were popping out from her neck. Her face was inflamed.

Samantha widened her eyes and acquired all her strength to push her aunt away. Evelyn fell to the floor after her head hit the corner of the platform. To double confirm her unconsciousness, the frightened lass lifted up her leg to snap Evelyn's neck. She was rather shocked by what she had been doing lately—pushing her aunt, snapping her neck—she was indeed proud. She got a head start to leave the house. Holding Nathan's hand tightly, she ran outside.

She ran, dragging along the clueless boy until a beautiful house attracted her. She rushed toward the doorstep and banged the door as if her life was at stake. Nathan innocently repeated her actions of slapping the door till it got received.

'Open the door!' Samantha cried.

On the other side, stood Elora. She received it with a frightened face. Samantha and Nathan slightly pushed the door inward and made their way inside the house. Elora firmly locked the door and she waited for an explanation.

'I'm sorry to barge in this way,' Samantha apologized. On getting no reply from Elora, she continued speaking. 'I am Samantha and this—this is my brother, Nathan. My mother left us with our aunt and she's behaving differently'

'She's a zombie!' Nathan joined, not knowing what those words meant.

'What's all that chaos?' Raghav rushed upstairs with a shot of vaccine. He noticed two strangers at his house and looked at Elora for an introduction.

'They were attacked by a zombie,' said Elora, in a low voice.

Raghav frowned. 'Elora, please. Kids, where would this attacker be right now?'

'Just a few blocks away. I think I broke her neck. It sounded like I broke her neck,' Samantha stuttered as she watched Raghav nod.

'I'll get some snacks and heat this pizza up for you.' Elora took the pizza box from her weak hands.

Samantha had never seen a staircase go downwards in a house. 'Where does that lead to?' They walked toward the couch and quietened their bodies.

'My morgue,' Raghav replied as he polished the needle.

'Why do you have that in your hand?'

'It's a shot in the dark.'

Samantha frowned. 'Wait, your morgue? You wouldn't happen to know any Aaron O'Malley, would you?'

'I think I do. John Doe that was brought to me a few days ago.' Raghav put a stop to his words as Samantha broke into tears.

Samantha needed her father. She forgot to grieve; it was hard for her to believe that her father was no longer alive to take over such tiring situations and calm them down. The low sob turned into a loud cry.

Raghav comprehended the cause of their distress. He looked away and mumbled, 'Aaron's kids.'

Chapter 17: Thoughts

Your brain is unstoppable. You're reading this and simultaneously thinking about an assignment that is due, probably a work that has to be finished before a given time. Your brain is scattered all around the place and it will not stop thinking until you're dead.

Gracy.

My body is ready to shut down. My brain can't take it anymore. I am Gracy Brown, youngest deputy superintendent of APD, yet I stand here, helpless watching my people die right before my weak, tired eyes. Problems never knock on the door, they barge in without a warning. I needed one day with Eric, was it too much to ask for? No, I'm not being selfish. I did not get to interact with my personal life for years.

Being a police officer, I have witnessed deaths. A lot of them. But never like these. Blight did not deserve to die this way neither did the crew members. And Maverick? He was killed because he wasn't strong enough to look at someone dying. Hendricks? He was killed because he could not hide his emotions. Are these really good reasons to die over, or are they actual reasons to die over?

I can only hear the cries of my people; my eyes are desperate to look at at least one of them. I don't have the energy to scream, others won't have the energy to reply back. Even if I did have the energy, my dry mouth would not be able to deliver the words. All I can do is wait but I need to know if they're OK. No, they're obviously not. What have I done? How could Erica do this? We trusted her. But I don't think she wants to do this anymore. She passed by four times and all the time, her eyes were scary. Who can blame her? She did not have a sane childhood. An island filled with lifeless yet dangerous creatures and a father who looked at her as a medium to get to us. I don't think I should stop believing in you. You have your reasons, everyone has got their own reasons. But taking it this far? A small heads-up would've been helpful.

My arms are numb. Wiggling doesn't help because I can't feel them anymore. My eyes are barely awake, they're terrified they are tired of watching people die. But they're brave. We have to fight.

I see Inhune smirking at my miserable state. Keep looking, I won't lower my eyes never in front of you.

Ugh, my stomach is growling. I need to crack my bones; they've never been this stiff. I want to scream, scream my lungs out but we are stuck in the middle of nowhere. No one's going to hear me. No one's coming to rescue us. We have to do it ourselves.

Disgusting! They're smiling and chewing human meat in front of us. A Fenjee just passed by with a hand he waved it in front of me, and I hid my retch. I know who it is. I saw Maverick's tattoo, oh Mave.

Eric might have figured that out too. I can't imagine what he must be going through right now. I should check on him, please reply.

'Eric?!' Gracy's dry voice tried yelling.

Eric.

I can hear you screaming my name, Gracy. Your desperate voice wants to know if I am OK or not but how can I reply? My lip muscles can't seem to coordinate with my voice. My skin is burning, and I need to itch every part of my body but I am tied up against the tree! What did I—

I want to tell her that I will be OK sooner or later but not now. Right now I can only think about Maverick. He was a part of my family. Yes Roger, I now know what you're going through.

These people don't care, they just slaughtered him and now they're eating him in front of us. I saw them take the body. I know it's him. They're loudly chewing on his meat with their filthy teeth.

I can't feel any part of my body, everything has died. I need Gracy. I need to see her. I miss her. Her face lit up when she gave that ring to me. As long as I know her, I'm sure she bought that ring way before I bought hers. A beautiful ring and that man is wearing it. He's wearing my ring. MY ring. It's not even about the ring anymore, it's that I was so weak that I couldn't protect it.

I need water. I can't move. There's no life left inside of me, my tears are over and my anger wants to take over but how? I am tied up and my friends died in front of me and I couldn't save them. My head hurts. I can't even think without my brain aching. STOP THINKING! I can't keep my eyes open for long. I can't do this.

Stop staring at me, Inhune. Smiling at my weakness. Laughing at my loss. I need my ring back pleading won't help. Yelling? He'll hurt me again but the ring is worth it but he won't give it to me. Gracy gave it to me with passion, and I couldn't hold on to it even for a day. I need to know how she is. I need to know how my parents are.

I shouldn't have agreed to come here. Half of the people here died because of me. There is no Fenjaitus. Of course, there isn't. Of course, I was blinded. I always wanted a little sister and I had her for a while. I had everything I ever wanted. How could she turn on us this way? I don't know who else to blame Erica? No. Inhune? My parents were the ones who ditched him. My parents? They didn't know what they were doing, they said they did it for me. Me? I can't blame myself, I was a small kid. I saw that guilt in Erica's eyes when she looked at me. I wish things were different. Is Gracy still waiting for a reply?

'Grace,' Eric whispered. It was loud enough to reach her ears. 'I'm here.'
'Eric,' she cried.
'I know I know.'

Emanuel.

I did this to my children. I am to be blamed. I should have known my brother better. How did I not grasp that this could be one of Inhune's traps? He was always this revengeful. Why did we have to complete the virus? But Inhune he manipulated me. And now, he's doing the same to Erica. Poor thing, I can only imagine what she had to go through.

Wait, is that? Dear motherland, they're eating someone's leg. Could it be Mave? He was a good lad. I still remember how he once called me 'Dad' by mistake. But then he felt good so kept calling me his dad. He's dead. What have I done? This is devastating.

I see you eyeing me Inhune. I know you're trying to make me feel guilty. I do. I feel guilty! This is my punishment. Take me. Why are you dragging everyone else in? Guess this brings you joy! It is my fault; I should have come back to save you.

My whole body feels rigid. I can feel my blood flow stop. It was my decision to leave them behind. I should be punished, no one else. No one else. And Abi

'Abi! Are you OK, my love?' asked Emanuel.

'I am,' she replied, weakly.

Abiyeth.

I say that I am OK but I am not. My body feels weak, but I can only think about Eric. We tried saving him from this island and here we are tied against these trees. Please protect us, motherland. We have done so much for Eric this cannot be it. It cannot end like this. There has to be something else.

I knew this virus was going to be harmful to all of us. I remember asking Emanuel to stop completing the virus. I'm sure we could have worked out some negotiations with the Nicodemus family. But of course, he listened to his dear brother. Inhune has always been like this. Manipulative. He has done that to me as well.

I was more happy than shocked when I met Erica—ouch my ankle! I robbed Erica of her childhood. That girl she's good. I know that because she is part of me. She is my child too. Even though I haven't known her for long I know she has a pretty soul.

'Erica, my lass!' Inhune exclaimed as he kept his hand on her head. 'I am sorry I spoke to you dismally. You're my good child, right?'

'Yes, Father.' She smiled.

'Very well would you be so kind as to fetch us some firewood?'

'Yes, Father,' her voice got dull. She walked toward the dense part of the island.

Erica.

"Yes, Father" can I not stand up for myself? What a liar he is. I know he doesn't think about my betterment. Does he think I'm a nincompoop? Am I saying that word a lot? Nincompoop. Nin—com—poop He's been doing this since I was

a kid but I am an adult now. Summer breeze huh? I know he butters me every time he needs something. He knows I won't refuse. I can't.

I show I fear nothing but I fear one thing. My father. His eyes boil whenever I rebel. I cannot deny the fact that I love putting wrinkles on that man's face. Satisfying. Growing up in Fenjiyawa, with him as my guardian, not easy. I was taught that people from the real world were heinous but not once did they treat me the way my father treated me.

I played them false and now they won't ever trust me again. Why would they trust me? I don't even trust myself anymore.

I have to do something. They don't belong here. My father does not deserve this satisfaction from hurting innocent people. I have to do something. Oh, I'm close to the fire wood.

'Hunter?' Linette yelled.

'Don't worry about me.' He tried responding.

Hunter.

I am barely alive. I can't feel any part of my body. The only thing keeping me alive is Samantha. I have a daughter that hates me and I have to make that right before leaving the world. My soul will not rest in peace until then. I may not match Aaron's level but I'll do anything to keep them happy.

Or maybe I should just forget about it, I don't think Linette wants me to come anywhere near her family. Ouch, ah! Cramp! That hurts! OK, breathe.

Much better. I can't believe this is happening. I can't even focus on my own thoughts! I have a kid. I have a goddamn kid! And I love Linette, I still love her but she's making it difficult for me to feel it.

I can't think right, I can't hear myself think. Am I even thinking? Am I hallucinating? Why is everything going to blur?

My throat is dry, I need water. I am weak. I hate being weak. This month hasn't really been in my favor. Wouldn't be surprised if I died here no! Why am I getting such thoughts? Right, this is it I am going crazy. But it can't end like this. Is anyone planning an escape? I can't really see anyone. It would only be decent if I asked Linette about her health.

'Lin—' Hunter gulped as he tried to yell.

'It's OK! Don't try to talk, I'm OK,' she replied with a calm voice.

Linette.

I can't imagine what he's going through. How cruel can someone be? Why are they doing this to us? There is no humanity here. But can I really blame them for what's happening? This island can make a sane go insane. It can't end here, I have to go home to my kids. I shouldn't have left them alone. I'm never going to leave them alone. Ugh, my arms are itchy. My kids must think I'm a terrible mother to leave them alone. I'm sure they're OK right, who am I kidding? They're with Evelyn, they hate her. I don't see why they hate her. She's a beacon of hope and she can be a real pain in the ass sometimes.

I miss Aaron. I shouldn't have been ignorant when his behavior changed and should have forced him to tell me what was happening. I love Hunter. Wait, where did that thought come from? No. Leave!

Good lord, I cannot feel my fingers or any part of my body. Everything's numb. I need water should I ask? I'd rather stay silent.

'Poppy, you alright?' Jacob yelled.
'Holding up,' Poppy replied.

Poppy.

Since when does he care about me? Oh god, what am I doing here? I don't belong here! I'm parched. We have to get out of here soon before they kill us all. It can't go down like this.

Hm, kinda felt nice when out of all, he asked me how I was holding up. Do I care for him? I'd never know. People are going to judge me if they know I—Poppy! Shut your brain!

'How about you Jacob?' she asked.
'Oh, I'm OK!' he exclaimed.

Jacob.

What? She asked me if I was OK? Maybe she's just being formal because I asked. Maybe it's because of my behavior toward her. Standing here being all tied up against a tree and waiting for my death just makes me realize how valuable life is. I wasted all my time lying to myself. Hm, when the officers said that they found Sophia did they mean they found her or her body?

'Alex! Buddy—' Marcos asked in a low voice as he knew Alexis was close by.

'Still alive!'

Marcos yelled out another name, 'Roger?'

'I'm great!' Roger passed a sarcastic, yet furious comment.

Roger.

No one. I have no one. No family. The only thing I had was my briefcase and now that's gone too. No one is alive. Everyone's dead and I am going to die here. This is it. Maybe coming here wasn't a bad idea after all. I couldn't have lived with myself, anyway, better just die out here where everyone else did. No one, I have no one. No one. Oh, Roger, you have given up on life, haven't you?

'Your firewood,' said Erica as she handed them over to Inhune.

'It took you longer than usual,' he suspected.

'Sorry, Father, a cage was open and a Zombie escaped.'

'A what?' Inhune had never heard that word before.

'A diseased man escaped,' she corrected.

'A diseased man got out?' He laughed aloud. 'Montgomery, you're lucky I'm in a good mood. Please be careful next time.' He stared at the abashed face of the man who was in charge of the cages.

Erica looked away and thought this better work.

Chapter 18: In the Memory Of

I'm sorry, but it takes love to sacrifice.

It's almost night. The bon fire started flaming out as the cold air started taking place. The wind howled uncontrollably. Lips were chapped and cries were inaudible. Throats were dry. Nothing but dark fate was visible. The cruelty of Inhune had taken over everyone's will to live. Not a muscle could be moved to rebel. Brains had collapsed due to the overload of pressure.

'Get up,' said a faint voice from the sky that belonged to a gloomy dream. 'Eric!' He realized it wasn't a dream. Eric started preparing himself for the wake. 'Quick!' exclaimed the impatient, loud, and clear voice.

Eric opened his eyes to Erica's hastiness. She waved her hand and tapped his cheeks. 'Erica?' He was righteously puzzled. He jolted upright when he heard faint noises of people screaming from far away. 'What is that noise?' He enquired as he watched Erica untie him to freedom. His blurred vision fixed itself. He felt every part of his body breathe. He was free and confused.

Erica passed on a copper mug, containing fresh water, to Eric.

'And why would I accept another drink from you?' He gulped his dry throat, knowing he really needed any liquid down his throat, be it poison.

'It's clear water!' she yelled in a hushed voice. She relaxed her body and looked at Eric with empathy. 'You need it.'

Eric swallowed the water with great effort until the peristaltic movement was back in rhythm. It was heaven on hell for that span of time. 'Thank you.'

'You people have to escape.' Her head wandered, inspecting if the coast was clear.

'What did you do? What is that noise?' The mayhem grew louder.

'It's the sound of Fenjees getting busy.'

'That's not what human mating sounds like'

'What are you talking about?'

'Oh, I forgot you're not caught up with the slangs yet.' Eric pushed himself to stand upright. 'Where are the island people?'

'The Fenjees are distracted but not for long. Help me untie everyone.'

Eric replied with an agreeing nod. Without further questions, he tried running toward Gracy whilst taking support from the trees in his way. He fell on the ground a couple of times before he got to her. 'My legs are numb.' He whispered to himself.

He walked up to Gracy's half-awakened face. Splashing water on her, he politely called out, 'Gracy?' He watched her face wrinkle as the water disturbed her rest. She felt water going down her throat as Eric tried holding back her head. After coming back into her senses, she shot her first question.

'Is this an escape?'

'It is.' Eric untied her.

Simultaneously, Erica freed Linette.

'There is good in everyone.' Linette's dry voice took over the silence.

Erica's lips twitched as she fought it with a smile. 'Untie Hunter.'

'Thank you.' Linette rushed toward Hunter with half-asleep legs, watching Gracy and Eric help the others out of the rope.

Hunter's body was unconscious. Linette started untying the knots while trying to get him back. On getting no response, she agitated and shook him strenuously while watching him slowly open his eyes. He growled in pain. 'What are you doing?' he stuttered weakly.

'It's me, Linette.' She wrapped his arm around her shoulders.

Everyone was surely out of the rope; however, they were trapped in weakness. Slowly, their legs started adapting to the actions of walking.

They gathered in a circle, waiting for an explanation.

Erica stepped forward and announced, 'Alright, an apology is in order. A simple sorry won't make up for the fact that half of you are dead and most of you are about to.'

'About to die?' Zachery panicked.

'Half of you look horribly sick right now.'

Eric interrupted, 'And who's fault is that?'

Erica replied with embarrassment, 'I am aware that this is my fault. I'm sorry. You don't have much time. Run straight from here, you'll find the ship unanchored at the shore.' She pointed at a clear path.

'You're coming too, right?' Abiyeth asked in concern.

'Someone has to hold these Fenjees back while you flee.'

'He'll kill you.' Gracy shivered.

'He's my father.'

'Regardless, he will kill you.'

After a dramatic pause, running footsteps were heard nearing. Erica nodded and justified. 'I brought you here. Now help me correct my mistakes and run. And be careful! I've set some traps, don't walk through them.'

'Come with us.' Eric shot his last chance.

'I will try my best.' She watched everyone hesitantly run in the direction of the ship, taking each other's support.

She turned around as the crackling fire flames approached her. The Fenjees were confused. Inhune was raged. He stared at Erica and stomped toward her. For the very first time, she did not flinch. She stared back at him with anger, trying to match his furiousness. This made Inhune boil more than ever.

'You think you can get away with this?!' Inhune yelled at her expressionless face.

'I don't care,' she whispered.

Inhune's face twitched. 'Where are they?'

'I don't know.'

'Where are they?' His heavy hand threw itself against Erica's neck as she firmly gripped it. He watched her choke, he couldn't seem to stop himself from doing so. His intentions were only to scare her; however, his rage exerted more pressure than he intended to apply. He watched her struggle quieten down as her face muscles showed no response. He gasped and left her as she dropped dead to the ground. He stepped back, there was a slight moment of regret. He heavily panted through his nose and looked at everyone's horrified faces.

'Find them!' he yelled.

The Fenjees took his orders and dispersed immediately.

Inhune looked at Erica and whispered to her still body, 'You did this to yourself,' trying to justify his actions to himself. He looked away and marched back into the woods.

Upon the realization of the empty environment, Erica opened her eyes and smiled at the gray clouds. 'Nincompoop.' She nodded, listening to the traps getting triggered by the Fenjees. She let out an evil laugh as she crossed her arms while resting them under her head.

Evidently, every event was getting executed as planned. After realizing the Fenjees were worse than the humans of the real world, she highly regretted her decision of bringing them back to the island. She mended her mistakes by carefully unlocking all the cages that trapped the diseased human beings, she knew their restless legs would sooner or later get themselves out of the cage and create beautiful chaos. The chaos would keep the Fenjees distracted from the humans tied against the trees.

She then quietly placed all human traps that she could now hear—a calm melody to her ears—the rustling of the tree branches that held the Fenjees in a net. Soon they would become the fresh meals of those who escaped from the cages.

Upon the realization of the traps, the free Fenjees stepped forward carefully, in search of those running toward the shop.

Meanwhile, the legs of the human beings from the real world did not slow down. They took each other's support and ran as if their lives were at stake—and they were.

'I see the ship!' Gracy yelled as everyone increased their pace.

They heard the number of footsteps increase—they were not alone. Gracy put a sudden stop to her legs as everyone followed her actions. She turned around and froze. Their others turned around only to find two familiar diseased men walking toward them as if they were left hungry for years. They took a few steps behind as they weren't armed enough to win the battle.

Roger, on the other hand, searched for a weapon—he had had enough of these creatures and it showed on his frustrated face. His eyes found a pointed spear lying on the ground, amongst the dry leaves. He picked it up and tightly gripped it around its wood, not caring about the splinters piercing through his skin. Why would he?

Taking a closer look at his rivals, Roger saw his family—Akshay and Jack. A shiver ran down his spine, there was a certain muscle in his hand that twitched. Roger had flashbacks of them screaming for help. He growled at his emotional pain and was done being the universe's troll. He was ready to face his nightmare. The word "scared" was not an option for him anymore.

Gracy grabbed a heavy rock and looked at Roger. 'Jack and Gale?'

'Akshay.' Roger's bold voice took over.

'You don't have to do this if you don't want to.' Gracy looked at the men getting closer as they all backed up.

'It has to be me.'

'On the count of three?'

He nodded his head and rolled a firmer fist around the branch.

'One.' He was to forget all his relations with them and end their lives.

'Two.' Their souls were lifeless.

'Three.' Jack growled with his half-destroyed cheek as Roger pierced his brain through his open mouth. His blood splattered all over Roger's face and not once did he flinch.

Simultaneously, Gracy held Akshay's neck and smashed the rock against his head. The hit was extremely powerful—she punctured her target. The sight was excruciating to watch.

The bodies dropped dead on the ground. Roger panted out loud and stared at them for a couple of seconds. However, they had no time to pay respect to the dead.

The group made another head start. After a few steps ahead, they met the unanchored ship that stood there to rescue them from Fenjiyawa.

An unstable thick rope ladder hung down the ship.

'That looks dangerous.' Poppy fought for breath as she coughed.

'Nothing is more dangerous than this place.' Jacob looked back at the island, giving it a last goodbye.

'I'll see if that thing is stable or not.' Emanuel immediately grabbed the sides and climbed up with shivery legs. His body trembled as strong winds swayed the ladder, but he reached his destination successfully.

'Only one at a time!' Emanuel called out from the ship. Abiyeth started climbing up with weak arms.

Amidst the silence, angry footsteps of the Fenjees started emerging from the woods. After a small amount of time, slashes against bodies were heard as bodies fell on the rough Earth.

Eric looked back and whispered, 'Erica.' After silence conquered the environment yet again, a loud cry was heard and he knew it was Erica's. The slaughtering has stopped. His smile wore off. His eyes were desperate to get a glance at her but the pitch-black island did not allow them in doing so.

Gracy called Eric out from the ship, he was the last one standing on the ground. 'Eric! Quick!' He looked at Gracy and hesitantly climbed up the ladder as he built up scenarios of Erica's death.

The group was on board.

'It's umm a small ship,' said Marcos as his eyes looked through the blueprint. 'Zachery, start the engine and I'll handle the wheel.'

Zachery looked at him with confusion, not knowing why their flee depended on him. It was a responsibility he did not want to take. However, he randomly switched on a few buttons and heard the motor. He was perplexingly proud of himself.

The ship faced the sea and sailed off. They were relieved but fear had become their companion. Their heads turned toward Fenjiyawa as it started shrinking away from them.

'We left her behind.' Eric stared blankly into the woods.

'Who did we leave behind?' questioned a voice from the back.

The group frowned and turned around to find Erica standing in front of them, carrying a partially torn green bag and a flare gun. She stood upright with a smirky grin.

Eric stood there as a proud brother. His heart felt lighter. He walked toward her and continued staring.

'Looking for resemblance?' Erica asked, playfully.

'I heard you scream.' Eric placed his hand on her cheek to feel her presence.

Erica pressed her lips in embarrassment. 'I ran into a spider web.'

'You screamed cause you ran into a spider web?' Emanuel asked for reassurance.

'Look.' She stepped back and justified herself. 'They're creepy.'

Everyone burst into laughter as Erica stood there, nodding as she pleasantly smiled. After a while, they all dispersed around the ship in groups to take in the fresh, free wind.

Linette walked toward Hunter. He had his arms rested on the front deck's railing, watching the calm waves. She stood beside him and nudged his weak hand off.

'Oops,' she said as he placed them back.

'So.' he turned his face toward her. 'What happens after this?'

'I was thinking you could answer that.'

'I don't know about you but I am going to sip Pina Colada by the beach.'

They chuckled as tension in the air vanished completely, forever.

'I was thinking,' Linette hesitated. 'Samantha and Nathan could use a father to spoil them. Hunter, you're a good man—you always have been. I understand if you don't want to come back but—'

Hunter silenced her stutter as he passionately went in for a kiss. He held her neck and frowned as he felt her lips. A kiss that he had longed for. A pleasant moment where they felt alive again. They pulled away from each other as their foreheads met. They closed their eyes to process the moment.

Three feet apart, Erica looked at them as she blurred out their background. 'That's beautiful—' Erica's vision swiftly focused back on the island as she caught sight of four Fenjees and Inhune standing on the shore, waiting to launch their arrows. She gasped and yelled, 'Watch out!'

Simultaneously, Inhune's command echoed till their ship, 'Now!'

The arrows flew through the air ruthlessly, showing no mercy to humanity.

Jacob stood in front of Poppy as a sharp arrow penetrated the wood behind them.

Hunter covered Linette as he held her arm and roughly pulled her toward him. His entire body protected her.

Four arrows missed their aim, whereas Inhune's arrow impaled straight through Hunter's skull. His last sight was Linette's petrified face and frightened eyes as he fell on the deck, dragging her down with him.

Inhune smirked with satisfaction and pulled another arrow against the string with all the power he possessed.

Erica lifted her right hand, pointing the flare gun at Inhune, gathering the courage to finish him off for good.

The father and the daughter released their weapons at the same time. The arrow and the bullet on fire traveled from one side to another. They stared at each other with raised weapons and rage. There was a hint of sympathy that came into realization in Inhune's eyes. He knew the arrow was reaching Erica, he knew the flare was reaching him. He did not move, a sense of self-pride made me stand on the ground. Diseased human beings were loose, he had lost Fenjiyawa, he had lost his daughter, and there was nothing left for him.

The arrow pierced through Erica's arm. The bullet went through Inhune's heart. His clothes flamed and his skin felt the aggression of his daughter. The father screamed as his lass mummed her pain and fell on the deck.

'Erica!' Eric shouted at the top of his voice. He knelt down and carefully placed her head on his lap.

Abiyeth rushed toward Erica and fell to the ground for her.

Gracy stood there in between Hunter and Erica. Her eyes shifted from one body to another as she decided to rush toward the alive one.

'Erica?' Gracy knelt down beside her and held the arrow.

'No! It's a medieval arrow.' Erica gulped in pain.

'Get me two small hollow rubber pipes.'

'Exactly.'

Poppy found two objects similar to what Gracy had asked for. She picked them up and tossed them to her. Gracy looked at Erica's wound and shivered. She shrugged away her tense brain and pulled apart the flesh around the arrow. She placed the hollow rubber substance into the sharp sides of the arrow in order to prevent it from tearing off Erica's flesh. She held the arrow and embraced Erica for a pain she had never felt before.

'Just do it.' Erica pressed her lips.

Gracy pulled the arrow as Erica yelped in suffering. The arrow slipped out of her arm easily, yet the distress she went through could not be put into words.

The arrow brought chunks of flesh clots along with it. Eric held the wound and applied pressure on it. Alexis found a first aid kit but did not know how to apply it to this situation. They looked at Linette for medical help; however, she was in shock.

'Don't look at her. The arrow wasn't deep enough,' Erica mumbled.

Eric gave her a clean napkin and asked her to keep it in her mouth as they applied to rub alcohol to the wound. She wasn't prepared for the extra pain she was about to feel. As the liquid touched her wound, her body seized with torment. 'What is that?' She spit out the napkin and cried out loud, her nerves popped out as she clenched her teeth.

The pain quietened as Poppy temporarily sealed it with cotton and bandages. Erica looked at her with teary eyes.

'Don't worry, brother. This will heal,' said Erica as she coughed. Her eyes moved toward Linette. 'That won't.'

Tears ran down Linette's cheeks unmanageably. She started blubbering as mucus started flowing out her nose. She fought for breath. She banged her fist against the deck as they bled with splinters. Her eyes could not move away from Hunter's dead body. She was exasperated, she held his body and bawled. It was a quick death in her arms.

After all he had been through, after all that he had survived, he ended up lying on the ground, motionless. The only movement his body had was Linette trying to shake him, hoping for him to respond.

Hunter looked forward to a better tomorrow, but the universe consistently had different plans for him. He was always deprived of a beautiful life. Was it his unfortunate fate or was it Linette's?

Chapter 19: Quest

You drop your ice cream after a long day and you stand there, watching it slowly melt into the ground as you curse your fate. The more you look at it, the more regret you feel. "What if I had just been more careful?"

"What if I hadn't reached out to my purse while holding the ice cream? I would have never dropped it." But this is just the ice cream we're talking about. What if someone you love is lying on the ground in front of you and there is nothing you can do about it?

It's dawn. The tides are low. The ship sailed along with the sea, calm as ever, as if she knew her sailors needed healing. A soft breeze blew as the sun painted the sky in charming colors. Nature was in peace, whereas the people witnessing it—weren't.

Hunter's body started decaying in front of Linette. A pungent smell of a human being rotting mixed itself with the essence of fresh water. His body laid there, stationery, untouched, under a silky white cloth that absorbed his blood.

Linette sat beside his body, resting her back on the railing, constantly banging the back of her head against it. Her cries would pause and resume every five minutes. She built an imaginary circle around her, refusing to step out of it and take care of herself. She knew his one-second death was going to leave a huge impact on her entire life. She was numb—mentally and physically. The rotting smell was not a bother to her. Her hands bled, but the pain was not a bother to her. Her eyes were swollen, and she was exhausted from the constant grief.

'Linette.' Gracy approached her with the leftover courage she had gathered.

She stopped banging her head as she heard a rescue voice. Her eyes looked at Gracy, emotionlessly. She waited for her to say something; anything that would make her feel better.

'Hunter Callahan was a good man. He'd always put everyone's health before him. Seeing you this way would've made him upset.' Gracy tried looking at the body, but couldn't. She lost an officer that day, a very determined one. 'He would want you to eat—'

'Leave me alone,' said Linette as her dry throat let out a harsh tone. She continued banging her head against the railing and watched Gracy hesitantly walk away.

Gracy picked up herself and stayed strong for others. She made it her responsibility to take care of everyone. She continued walking toward a thin passage, in search of Erica's room. During the short walk, Gracy's brain started stimulating emotions. Her throat felt as if it was held against a cactus and she did not let tears roll down.

She walked past an empty conference room. Not far away from there, she passed by a restaurant where everyone only stared at their food.

Poppy and Jacob fidgeted with their sandwiches but did not dare to take a bite.

Roger had made himself comfortable toward the corner. It was as if he needed some time alone but was too afraid to not have company. He closely held his briefcase, chanting mysterious words to himself.

Zachery, Alexis, and Marcos gathered around a map, figuring out in which direction to take the ship.

She stepped down through a small ramp as doors to their respective rooms were located. 103—this is her room, she thought to herself. She took a deep breath and once she had opened the door, she was to mask her emotions.

She found Erica sound asleep and Eric sat on a chair beside her, restlessly shaking his right leg.

'Did she not wake up?' Gracy asked in concern.

'No,' Eric replied as he crossed his arms to feel the warmth on his fingers.

Erica opened her eyes without stress and looked at Gracy. 'I've been awake.'

Eric bolted upright with a startle and waited for an explanation.

'What was I to talk about?' She stopped for a cough. 'How I failed you?'

'You saved us,' Gracy rectified.

'Yeah, who took you there in the first place?'

'We needed the vaccine.'

Eric scoffed and joined the conversation. 'Then I believe it was a pointless trip because we lost more than we gained on that island.'

'Mother nature, good on you for reminding me about that.' Erica stretched her left arm to reach out for her backpack. It was shabbily placed on the side table.

She passionately dug inside and removed a huge ancient, wooden box. She slid off the lid and revealed precisely a hundred liquid tubes containing gray liquid.

Gracy stepped forward in amazement. 'Don't tell me that's the—'

'Antidote,' Erica beamed.

'I thought Inhune said there was no vaccine.'

'Evidently, my father was a liar.'

Eric quietly heard the conversation. He could not show any spirit.

'Maverick is in a better place now,' Erica consoled.

'Inside the Fenjees' stomach is a good place for his corpse to chill?' He scoffed.

'He won't be in there for long,' she said in a low voice.

Gracy widened her eyes and nodded, indicating it wasn't the right time to joke around. Eric looked at Erica and diverted his vision toward the wall as he pinched his forehead.

'You should rest,' said Gracy.

'I brought back something you possessed.' She, again, dug her hand inside the backpack and searched for the ring.

'Here.' She removed it and placed her hands in front of him. He bolted upright and slightly snatched the ring from her hand. Gracy raised her eyebrows and smiled. Her eyes moved to Eric's relief. He slipped it back onto his finger and stared at it as Maverick's death replayed in his memory.

A phone call ruined the silence. Gracy frowned. 'Who's phone is that?'

'I've never owned one,' Erica whispered as she shrugged her shoulders.

Eric opened the drawer and recalled, 'This was Linette's room.'

The call was from an unknown number, he grabbed the phone and kept the call on speaker. 'Hello?' asked a desperate voice from the other side.

'Um, hi. This is Officer Brown, who are—'

'Gracy? Where's Mom?'

'Samantha?' She walked toward the phone.

'Where is my mother?'

'She's resting. Where are you calling from? Aren't you with your aunt?'

'About that, Gracy, my aunt is a Zombie. Things are getting worse out here! The number of guards is decreasing. I don't think we're safe anywhere. I had to run away from her house and—'

'Slow down! Where are you right now?'

Samatha looked at Raghav and asked, 'Excuse me, sir. What exactly is your name?'

Raghav, while injecting Elora with the vaccine, replied, 'Dr. Raghav Campbell.'

'At Dr. Raghav Campbell's house.'

Upon hearing his name, Eric snatched the phone from Gracy and removed the call from the speaker. 'Give it to him.' He spoke into the microphone.

Samantha stretched her arm and handed the phone to Raghav.

His confused, hesitant hands took the phone from her.

'Yes?'

'Dr. Campbell!'

'Eric? Eric! Where the hell are you? Why are you with this child's mother?'

'Long story, sir. You have to hear me out, you very well know that I do not totter nonsense.'

'Try to convince me, Eric.'

'I have the vaccine for this virus. It'll take us three days to reach there, you need to try and keep it all under control.'

'Three days? Where are you coming from?'

'An island,' he stuttered. 'Just know that we can stop what is happening.'

'Where there's a virus, there's a vaccine. Wait, does that mean Maverick and Hendricks are with you? Because they're unreachable too—'

'They were with me but they couldn't make it.' Eric paused.

Raghav did not want to burden him with questions. 'We'll talk about it when you come back.' He cut the call and took a long breath, thinking about what could have happened to two of the most incredible men.

Eric kept the phone aside and started mulling over the horrifying events.

'Eric?' Gracy interrupted.

Eric looked at her furiously and yelled, 'They're effin' dead!'

Gracy gasped and froze.

Erica looked at her and said in a calm tone, 'Just step back. It's the virus talking.' They stayed still until Eric got a sudden jerk of realization. He watched their scared faces. 'W-why does it feel like this has happened before?' he panted.

'It has,' Gracy replied.

'The vaccine in you is fighting the virus. You'll keep losing yourself for a few minutes but I promise it will go away soon,' said Erica.

'If you say so.' Eric seated himself in shock.

'The virus never takes over the antidote. Although, we must pray that it does not develop. If it does, we'll have to create a stronger vaccine.'

Chapter 20: Jasmine

A normal human being can hear up to only 20,000Hz and any frequency above that is just a silent catastrophe.

Three days later.

The state needed the vaccine more than ever as the virus had become unstoppable. People were in a state of misery with masks and gloves coming back into existence. This virus was like no other. It knew how to control the entire human brain and destroy everything that came in its way. A chaotic atmosphere took place when street guards were brutally butchered by a group of infected people. It started building its own species, the rotters.

Gracy and Eric were standing on the far end of the ship, silent as the sea as they had found a big wooden box, enough to fit Hunter in it earlier that morning. Linette's blubber was still heard to the ends of the sea.

Zachery, on the other hand, ran toward them bearing good news. 'We see a land! It has to be Annapolis.' He took them to the front deck.

The sun shone brightly above them without mercy, resulting in them shading their eyes with cupped hands. They all glanced at the land skeptically.

'Where are your binoculars?' Zachery asked Gracy.

'Island, I suppose,' she replied. 'We won't really know if that's Annapolis till we reach the land.'

Eric exhaled air through his mouth in melancholy. 'I should go check on my parents.' He walked away, leaving Gracy with Zachery to watch the land get closer in hope.

Abiyeth and Emanuel were inside a room, trapped in a cassette that played all the terrifying incidents again and again. Their hands were cold, their teeth quivered, yet their bodies were motionless.

Abiyeth looked at the slow opening door and prepared herself to face a conversation. 'Eric.' She weakly pushed herself away from the head board.

He shut the door and stood by the dressing table, facing his parents. He watched Emanuel slightly scratch his shoulder, where Inhune had left his handprints.

Emanuel detested Inhune for what he did, however, he was once a supporting brother. He was never harsh toward his own family. The only thing that had made him ruthless, was Emanuel's escape with Abiyeth and Eric—he did not know which brother was at fault.

For a few minutes, they let silence take over. However, Emanuel's words broke it. 'We warned you, Eric. We warned you about the island,' said his dry voice.

'Em!' Abiyeth exclaimed. 'Eric, it's not your fault, OK?'

'There we go, yet another mother-son moment! It's my fault.' Emanuel's voice took a louder tone. 'Inhune lies dead on the island which now makes me responsible for this virus!'

'Dad,' Eric affirmed. 'Erica brought back the vaccine.'

Abiyeth gasped at his words. 'Did she, now?'

'Annapolis must have been a hell hole by now,' said Emanuel, showing absolute zero ambition to the news.

Back at Annapolis.

At Dr. Campbell's place, everyone had gathered around in the living room, munching on leftover snacks and discussing the current situation.

'So, my mom really was on an island?' Samantha asked.

'It appears to be so,' Dr. Campbell replied.

Their small talks were distracted by loud distant noises. It caught everyone's attention. 'What's that?' asked Noah as he disgustedly stuffed his mouth with soggy fries.

'Let me check it out,' said Dr. Campbell as he rose up from his seat.

'Raghav!' Elora looked at him worriedly.

'Just a little peek through the window, honey.'

He walked up to the window, placed beside the main door. His head toward the right, everything seemed peaceful and quiet there. However, upon panning his head to the left, he witnessed around fifteen individuals, walking in groups, carrying an ax with fresh blood. A bunch of furious men marched on the street in the distance. As they passed by every house, a person got separated from the group and barged into someone else's property. They started slaughtering random people and raided their houses—for a thrill.

Raghav froze. He started studying their behavior and came to the conclusion that they were not those ordinary serial killers. Their faces had turned pale yellow and something about them just did not seem humane. One of them caught Dr. Campbell peeping out the window. They stared at each other, the man smiled at him and raised his ax, indicating that they were next.

'Dad?' Noah called him out.

'Uh.' Raghav immediately separated himself from the window and looked at Elora. He quickly inclined his vision to his morgue and repeated his actions twice, specifying that they had to go into hiding. Elora opened her eyes wide and nodded lightly as she knew the bodies and the faint smell would not be a pleasant environment for the kids.

'What's happening?' Samantha joined the conversation.

Elora knew only the worst of the worst situations would force Raghav to take the decision of taking them into his morgue. 'You go first in and clean up that filthy place!' She watched Raghav rush downstairs to adorn the floor.

He entered the ground floor and hastily locked the morgue doors. He removed his old air freshener and sprayed it in the passage to cancel out the horrendous smell of the rotting bodies. He took a long breath as he was about to reveal his secret lab, a metal door that was placed at the end of the long passage. He walked toward it and placed the card with his hand over the scanner.

A red light scrutinized his brave eyes. The metal door opened to a small cabin with bright lights, followed by a clear glass door. 'State your name,' said a calm female robotic voice.

'Dr. Raghav Campbell,' he stated his name proudly. The frequencies of his voice reached the microphones, placed on the two diagonal sides of the small cabin, and the glass door opened, with a highly exerted air pressure.

'Welcome Dr. Campbell,' said the voice as the room lit up with white spotlights.

'Elora!' he called out at the top of his voice.

A faint call was heard. Elora took a deep breath. 'Now, we are going to hide down there, OK?'

'Who are we hiding from?' Noah asked.

'From people it's a game.' Elora stressed the last word, signaling Noah to stop asking questions she could not answer in front of Arabella and Nathan.

'Oh,' understanding the signal, 'Fun!' He smiled at Arabella and Nathan.

'Yay!' exclaimed the innocent children.

They rushed downstairs and entered the morgue. Elora firmly closed the heavy steel slab, securing the ground floor. Everyone sniffed the strong smell in the air.

'What on Earth?' Noah tried holding in his vomit.

'That's bad.' Samantha pinched her nose.

'It's his stupid air freshener,' Elora mumbled in irritation. The strong air freshener's aroma mixed itself with the pungent smell of the bodies to create the ghastliest stench anyone could ever smell.

Samantha knew her father was in one of the rooms. Her eyes could not wait to catch the last glimpse of his body. She slowed down her legs and watched the others go forward. She gulped while holding on to the right room's doorknob. Her hands twisted the handle but the door was jammed, she was somewhat relieved.

The noise of this activity grabbed Elora's attention. She turned back and looked at Samantha with her commiserating eyes. She walked toward her and held her hand. 'Later, you have my word,' she promised Samantha.

Samantha pressed her lips and left the doorknob. She felt Elora's caring hand take her toward the secret room.

The odors shifted to a comparatively pleasant smell. They were awestruck the moment they entered the room. It was as if the walk to this room was time travel—they had entered the future. An enormous area that carried loads of unseen inventions. Around ten to fifteen computers attached to the left side of the wall were connected to a master control system. An exhibition of technologies on the right side and blue prints of all kinds lay on the table in front of them.

Once everyone had stepped inside the room, Dr. Campbell pushed a red button installed beside the glass door. The doors shut themselves firmly followed by a sudden release of oxygen from the ceiling.

'Welcome to my creation.' Raghav smiled at the admiring faces.

'What have you been hiding from us?' Elora asked in fascination.

'All my work. If you think you've married only a Pathologist, you're wrong. I create things that are beyond everyone's imagination,' he stammered. 'W ell, this generation is smarter than I expected so, not really beyond anyone's imagination but—'

'What does this do?' Samantha stroked a matte black device.

'Don't!' Raghav yelled but lowered his voice. 'Touch that. It's a microscope.'

'I hate to break it to you but that's already been invented.' Samantha smiled.

'Child.' Raghav tried keeping his cool. 'That microscope is not your daily regular. Once you place a specimen under it, the microorganism is studied by my device and displays the same specimen, larger, in three-dimensional. It projects in the glass case next to it—a hologram. And when that has been projected, all the information about the virus shows up on the computer next to it. I just have to push one button for all that to happen.' Raghav stood there, looking at everyone's mesmerized faces.

'Does it work?' Samatha raised her eyebrows.

'Do you have a brain?'

'Duh?'

'Does it work?'

'OK, so let's try this device!'

'Please, do not go anywhere near my devices, they're very delicate.'

'What do all these computers do?' Elora interrupted before Dr. Campbell blew up.

'This is the best part,' Raghav showed excitement. 'Elora, turn on my spy station.'

'What do you mean? I'm supposed to know this? I don't know how to.' Elora was confused.

She was interrupted by a sensual robotic voice, 'Your wish is my command, Dr. Campbell.'

Raghav burst into a snorting chuckle as he explained.

'I programmed her this way. I figured—why not have at least one Elora that listens to me?'

Elora threw a sarcastic laugh, 'Interesting, you're cheating on me with a voice.'

The screens gradually lit up from left to right, neatly, without any glitches. All the astonished eyes were on the monitors. It showed several footage of the surveillance cameras installed inside and outside their villa.

Their smiles dissipated as they witnessed a bunch of furious individuals halting outside their house. A furious man separated himself from the group and entered their front gate, making way into their house.

Noah covered Nathan's eyes, and Samantha covered Arabella's.

'Raghav,' Elora whispered in horror. She did not know what was happening.

However, Dr. Campbell put on a calm mask. 'He can get inside the house but not this room. He has to pass a lot of security systems to reach here, not to mention the heavy steel door. This room is soundproof, a normal human being cannot listen to whatever goes on here even if he puts his ears against the door.'

'He does not look like a normal human being to me.' Elora held his coat.

The man looked to see as if he was ready to kill. He bit the empty air and seemed impatient. His body language was unusual. He shook his head and panted loudly through his nose as his body kept turning pale yellow. He took a step back and raised his ax in order to slash the door. He managed to break the lock, a firm kick opened the door wide allowing him to invade the property.

Elora and the kids were shivering with fear as the atmosphere got intense. Their eyes stuck on the live security footage, closely watching the man's every move.

'Where are you?' The man called out as his voice started getting rough.

'He's saying something.' Elora pointed out.

Dr. Campbell increased the volume as the cameras picked out the man's audio.

'I can smell you, Jasmine.' He was tempted to run his ax through someone's body.

Nathan whimpered lightly. Noah gasped and covered Nathan's mouth in order to not be heard by the ruthless man.

'It's alright.' Dr. Campbell looked at Noah. 'They can't hear us.'

'They can't hear us!' The furious man imitated, loudly.

Dr. Campbell's ears were still. He looked back at the screen and was petrified. In spite of all the security, they felt unsafe. Their only last hope was the steel slab standing as a barrier.

The man climbed downstairs and reached the slab. He frowned and started entering a code. Dr. Campbell's heart stopped, he wondered if the man really knew the code to the door. However, to his relief, the man was just bluffing. Raghav sighed in relief and looked at Elora. 'There's no way he can get through.'

'You said he couldn't hear us either' Elora sobbed.

The furious man got irritated and started randomly clicking on the numbers. When nothing worked, he started banging the steel door with his ax. He shouted out random words and created dents on the slab.

Elora's lips quivered as she wrapped her arms around both her kids, while Samantha knelt down to hug Nathan's terrorized body.

The system felt threatened and an alarm went off along with the robotic voice that stated every five seconds, 'Red alert.' People inside the room didn't even feel the loud siren; however, the man outside threw his ax at the door with rage as he screamed and held his ears. The siren was affecting him as loud frequencies reached his ears.

'He's running away?' Raghav seemed confused, trying to take over the chaotic noise. 'Elora!' Raghav raised his voice. 'Elora, turn off the system!' At his command, the place was quieted down. Raghav's eyes turned to the screens and found no intruder. The man was gone.

'They hear ten times louder than what we hear,' Noah concluded, watching Raghav breathe through his mouth, confused.

'Not only can they hear ten times louder but also smell ten times more,' Elora stuttered in shock. 'He said Jasmine, I'm—'

'You're wearing the Jasmine scent I gifted you.' Raghav connected the dots and watched Elora's scared face.

'How did he pass that horrible odor and specifically smell the Jasmine?' Samantha questioned.

'Maybe they can filter the things they want to,' Noah added.

'Makes sense,' Samantha replied.

Ignoring the children's senseless conversation, Raghav mumbled to himself, 'All their senses have been enhanced. The virus seems to be developing beyond our capabilities.'

Chapter 21: Unanswered Questions

Rewind. Your school bus doesn't arrive at all and you're late for school. The first lecturer is not easy to convince. How would you make her believe in your story? This is just school, the worst that could happen would be you being sent back home or is it the best? Anyway, what would you do if you were to get arrested if not successful in convincing?

Not more than two days later, the land was visible. To their surprise, they were successful in getting their ship back to Annapolis. Just a few more waves and they were about to reach their homeland with the vaccine.

Gracy noticed some angry man, all suited up, standing on the wet sand to receive the sailors. Everyone gathered toward the beginning of the ship and looked at each other.

'You know who they are?' asked Emanuel to Gracy.

'FBI.' Gracy sighed in frustration.

The ship took over the shore as Gracy immediately threw down the unstable ladder. She let herself climb down as everyone followed her.

Linette, on the other hand, needed a few more minutes before she could say her goodbyes to Hunter.

Gracy dusted off her shoulders and stood up straight in front of the men, looking eye-to-eye, not once did she blink.

'The infamous Officer Brown.' A manly voice laughed as it walked toward her.

'Agent Arthur,' she boldly greeted him. 'To what do we owe the pleasure?'

Their acquaintance had occurred a long time ago. They've worked together many times to come to an understanding that they absolutely detest each other. Working on something and agreeing with one another never really happened.

Agent Arthur kept trying to sabotage her career by stealing all her cases and pointing out all her little mistakes in front of a whole crowd. Gracy never believed in the word "nemesis" till he happened to her life.

'Received an anonymous tip of a ship sailing illegally out of this country. I didn't know it was you until this very second! You know, I'm not surprised, you've always been a reckless lil' bird.'

'Hey, watch it,' Eric warned.

'I do not have to explain myself to you, Agent.' Gracy looked straight into his eyes.

Agent Arthur slightly tilted his head and squinted his eyes. He was furious to hear her degrade him in front of everyone. He relaxed his face into a smirk and announced, 'I claim jurisdiction.'

'Since when?' Zachery joined the conversation.

James had a psychotic subtle grin. 'Since the time you violated the state laws. Now, explain yourselves or I will have to make several arrests and that's a lot of paperwork that we are trying to avoid but still wouldn't really mind.'

'You can't just claim something.'

'I see one person injured here, tell me there's no dead body in that ship and I'll let you go.' Agent Arthur placed a very generous deal.

'That happened outside this country,' Alexis asked.

'Then why'd you bring it back?' Agent Arthur smiled at Gracy and waited for her to start speaking.

Gracy sighed and looked at him with hopelessness, knowing that someone like him would never believe her story. She had to pick her words right, or she would've jeopardized everyone's life.

At Raghav's place.

Terrified faces took over the futuristic room. Looking at the screens made them witness some disturbing images, and closing their eyes only replayed the incidents.

Dr. Campbell's eyes moved left to right, watching the monitors, scanning for any intruder. 'They're gone,' he confirmed.

'Good,' said Elora as she casually wandered around the room.

'El, no. I know that walk, you're trying to make yourself comfortable, but don't. We need to get out of here right now.'

'What do you mean? I'm not leaving this room, or even making the children leave this room until a rescue team arrives.'

'Honey,' Dr. Campbell pressed his lips, 'This room is almost out of oxygen.'

Elora looked at him with despair, 'This room lacks oxygen? This room? I haven't seen anyone so intellectual yet so foolish—'

Before she could say more, Dr. Campbell politely justified himself, 'I keep the tanks limited so that I don't pressure myself to work here all the time. I really forgot ab—'

'You need a better system!'

'What we need is to get out of here. Anyway, it's no good staying down here, waiting for death to get us,' said Samantha while taking a bit off of her pizza slice.

'Quite tough to hear your murmur behind that slice but you're right.' Dr. Campbell watched her, trying to hide his disgust. He shuddered at the cheese stuck to her teeth and continued, 'I have something in here that will keep us safe. But before I reveal the gadget, know that I keep it only for emergencies—this seems to be one. And.' He looked at Elora. 'No questions will be answered.'

He walked toward a small microphone emerging out of a desk and whispered into it. 'Elora, open my secret cabinet.' He had no intention of saying it out loud to the room.

'Opening secret cabinet,' the robotic voice announced out loud.

'Shh! Keep it down!'

'Sorry, are you sure you want to open it?' the robotic voice whispered back.

'Yes, I'm sure.'

'For real?'

Dr. Campbell chuckled nervously and turned around to reveal confused faces staring at him. 'I entered this in my system to rethink my decisions. Elora, for real! Open the cabinet.'

'Access accepted. Opening file cabinet,' said the robotic voice as a small portion on the wall lit up. They watched a tiny door emerging out as a gadget sat there, untouched for months.

The Ruger SR 40s—one of the most dangerous hand pistols to ever exist. It's backed by a .40 S&W round with a caliber deadlier than a nine-millimeter.

'Dad!' Noah exclaimed in astonishment.

'Raghav!' Elora's voice took a high-pitched tone.

'It was my father's! I don't even know how to use it.'

'That's surely comforting,' Sarcasm intended.

On re-checking all the monitors once again, he found nothing to be suspicious about. Dr. Campbell took a deep breath and pulled the bolt, resting his finger on the trigger.

'Keep it off the trigger,' Elora warned, calmly, as she watched him take his finger off of it. He exhaled air through his mouth and pushed a red button to open the doors.

'Until next time, Dr. Raghav Cambell,' said the robotic voice as the real Elora rolled her eyes.

He stepped out first, carefully, as the other followed his every move. Steps up the stairs were taken fearfully.

They climbed up the last step and gathered in the living room. Meanwhile, Dr. Campbell reached out to the open door, trying to breathe as quietly as he could. He held the damaged door and pushed it until it stopped moving forward. He slightly gasped and left the handle to look at the obstacle.

To his fear, a furious man's leg got in the way. He kicked the door wide open as Dr. Campbell ran a few steps behind, holding the gun to his head level, shivering as his finger touched the trigger.

'Listen, just leave us alone. I have a gun and I will use it if I have to.' Raghav's voice did not tremble.

'But again, Dr. Campbell, you don't know how to use it, do you?' The man smiled sinisterly, enjoying the scared faces. 'We're going to torture you just like you tortured us.'

They watched eight people backing up the man with their ax. One of the men aggressively smashed the door with his ax, creating a terrifying environment as the other men laughed and walked toward Dr. Campbell.

Nathan and Arabella got startled as they cried out loud. Their sharp cry got into the men's ears as they flinched and covered their ears.

Dr. Campbell took this as an opportunity to open fire. He shut his eyes as tightly as possible and blindly shot a bullet. More than one shot was heard and the bodies dropped dead on the ground.

'Um, how many bullets does this gun shoot out at once?' Samantha asked in shock.

Dr. Campbell frowned and examined his gun skeptically. 'Just one.'

On lifting up his head, he saw a familiar face walking toward him, dogging the bodies on the ground. 'Eric Ainsworth!' he yelled in excitement and laughed in relief as they dramatically got saved.

Except for Roger and Eric's parents, the entire group showed up at Dr. Campbell's door. For once, he wasn't quite grumpy to have a large number of people at his place.

'Mommy!' Nathan yelled as he ran toward Linette. She knelt down and took him in her arms and teared up. She kissed him several times and looked at Samantha's relieved face. They exchanged pleasant smiles.

Eric walked out to Dr. Campbell. They looked at each other in silence, mourning the dead. 'What happened on that island, Eric? How did they die? Did the virus get them?' he asked in curiosity. Surely, it was tough to process the death of his two determined investigators.

'Let's just say that the island wasn't quite welcoming,' Eric replied in a low voice.

'The same island this virus came from?'

'Your patient zero—Aaron O'Malley—that's where he got it from.'

'Dr. Campbell,' Gracy unknowingly interrupted their conversation. 'Officer Brown.' She introduced herself and shook his hand.

Raghav looked at her with a subtle smile. 'Of course. The famous Gracy Brown! I've read a lot about you—'

'Alright!' James interfered out of jealousy. 'These unnecessary small talks never get over.' He looked at Dr. Campbell.

'Oh,' he said as his eyebrows shot up. 'Agent James, what a pleasant surprise. Welcome to my house.' He watched Agent James walk past them, ignoring his greetings.

Some made their way to the couch, others found a wall to lean on.

Eric looked at Dr. Campbell and stated, 'We have the vaccine, is it possible to make more?'

'Do you have enough for this whole city?'

'You tell us.' Eric looked at Erica as she handed over the wooden box to Dr. Campbell.

'And who is this lass?' Dr. Campbell looked at Eric for an introduction.

Erica joined the conversation and spoke of her own identity, 'Erica Aristarchus Eric's younger sister—a legacy of Fenjiyawa.'

'Same mother, different fathers messed up,' Eric added.

'Aristarchus' Raghav re-called out loud, 'Aristarchus! Like the legend of Nicodemus the tenth, where Aristarchus was a piece of sh—'

'No no, that's not right,' Eric's voice took a suppressive tone.

'Why not? Aristarchus really was a piece of shit.' Erica smiled.

'Interesting,' Dr. Campbell admired. 'So what you guys are their legacy?' He laughed innocently. For him he had cracked a joke, for the others it was an unfortunate fact.

'We are.' Eric pressed his lips.

'I've read about the tale of Aristarchus.' Dr. Campbell was fairly shocked, 'My father used to read it to me and said one day, if I'm determined enough, I'll find it. The funny thing is I've been searching for it since I was a kid and now it just walked toward me.' He was lost in a memory lane. No matter how much he tried drowning in them, he'd always come back into his senses within seconds. 'Well, Aristarchus huh?' He scoffed and nodded his head.

'Funny world,' Erica added with a confused smile, trying to study his serious behavior. 'So you've researched about my island?'

'Alright, island girl, let's just get to the damn point!' the agent yelled.

'Agent Arthur, calm the hell down,' Gracy defended.

'I won't. Is there anything you can do about it?'

'James, apologize to our women,' Eric added.

Agent Arthur laughed. However, watching Eric's face burn with anger, his smile mellowed down. Eric held his collar firmly and scowled. He could see his arrogant soul through his eyes and for the first time, felt scared of something. There was tension in between the two bodies, an unstoppable rage. Gracy held herself back and waited for Eric to get back into his senses.

There was no flicker of realization. The anger had become a part of Eric's body. He smirked and released his hand from the collar, knowing he was setting a bad example for the kids in the room.

'I will not tolerate any more nuisance in my house!' Dr. Campbell stepped forward. 'Agent Arthur, show yourself out.'

James scoffed while fixing his shirt. He rushed outside while still staring at Eric, hoping to get his vengeance soon. He got into his car and pushed the accelerator, having no destination in his mind.

'Dr. Campbell, one of my officers couldn't make it either. Is there an empty cabin in your morgue for him to rest?'

'Of course,' he replied in a dull voice. 'Number five. You can take him there.' He tossed the keys to Alexis. The boys disappeared for a while, trying to get the body inside the morgue through a back door.

Erica looked at Dr. Campbell and assured him. 'This antidote is extremely strong. One dose is enough for a person to develop the antibodies.'

Dr. Campbell opened the box and revealed tubes of gray liquid. 'This must be enough for the whole city.' He removed a tube and carefully lifted it up to his eyes level, admiring it. 'What is in this?'

Erica sat up straight, still weak from the wound, and handed him a piece of old paper. It was completely torn but the words were alive. 'The ingredients.'

Eric raised his eyebrows and was impressed, but not quite enough to show it.

'Yes, I can recreate this,' Dr. Campbell said proudly. 'It's an intranasal vaccine.'

'Doesn't matter how you take it.' Erica relaxed her body.

'It'll be easier for the people to take it themselves, and it requires a lesser amount of dose.' Dr. Campbell stared at the vaccine for a little longer. 'Stage one,' he recalled. 'A man is infected but not inhuman yet—they can be saved. Stage two he is inhuman, goes violent—he can't be saved, can he?'

'Oh.' Erica clicked her tongue. 'Dr. Campbell, just when I thought you were almost catching up on this virus. You see, stage two can be saved.'

'But the virus already takes over the body.'

'You're underestimating our vaccine. This is not the real-world vaccine we're dealing with—'

'Neither is the virus from our real-world that you keep talking about. It's highly advanced and it will keep developing.'

'You're forgetting where I come from, Dr. Campbell.'

'I've been in this career since you weren't even born.' Dr. Campbell looked at her. 'But you could be right.' He stalled the words but everyone heard it alright.

She shrugged her shoulders and felt a sense of triumph in the air, cheering Erica's name as she laid back, proud as ever.

'I have more disposable nasal sprays than I can count. Who's going to volunteer for the first and only dose?' Dr. Campbell looked around the room.

'I'll go first.' Gracy stepped forwards as she watched Dr. Campbell fetch a bunch of syringes.

He carefully emptied the tube, containing the vaccine, into a beaker and prepared a syringe for Gracy. He looked at the liquid and his shaky hands as he had never injected anyone with a vaccine he hadn't created.

He slightly pushed back Gracy's head and immediately sprayed the liquid into her nose. She flinched and sneezed out loud as she felt the liquid tickle her insides. She sucked in some of her mucus and rubbed her nose. 'That felt good.'

They waited for a few minutes, if Gracy survived the next ten minutes without pain, the vaccine would gain their trust.

'I feel fine,' said Gracy as she watched everyone closely staring at her face.

'Hit me up.' Poppy stepped forward and took the vaccine.

Person by person, the entire room got vaccinated, except for one—Dr. Campbell.

'Doctor, what about you?' asked Eric.

'What I just witnessed was insane. Looking at this list of what was put into the vaccine, I'm sure it will work. But my immune system is top-notch, so I'll pass on this one.'

'You can't just pass,' Samantha commented.

'I'm old enough to know what I can and cannot handle.' Dr. Campbell looked at Eric and asked, 'What are you thinking, Eric?'

'Alerting the health authorities won't do any good—'

'Because they would never believe you.'

'What if you spoke to them?'

'I'm not on good terms with those people, they're all too dumb for me.'

'You all possess the same level of degree.'

'Not the same level of brains.'

'Fair enough. What do you suggest?'

After a pause, Dr. Campbell threw a playful smirk and replied, 'Let's go rogue.'

Chapter 22: Hope

Day 1—there's a new virus in your town. Day 41—they find a vaccine. Would you trust your authorities and take the antidote?

Dr. Campbell brought down one of his highbrow creations—a medium-sized gray computer that seemed pretty outdated.

'This device,' he started explaining. 'Will activate any drone in the range of fifty kilometers. It will scan all the camera-fitted drones within its radar and activate them. They will start working on my command after that.'

'That's impressive. Does it require any particular type of make?' Eric stepped forward, examining the device.

'Good question. No, it does not.'

'Well, fortunately, there was a drone exhibition last month. They displayed around forty drones.'

'What are the odds?' Dr. Campbell looked at Eric and let out a laugh.

Jacob pressed his lips and joined the conversation. 'Spreading the news is going to be a tough task. I mean, people won't simply take the vaccine without any credible source telling them that it's alright to take it.'

'Except that they will have a credible source.' Gracy had been quite familiar with the area's most popular radio jockey—Millie Wilson. 'Citizens look for news updates on their radios, let's give them one.'

The entire plan had to be executed in a reduced amount of time. The idea of what was going to happen sounded pretty authentic to the people—it triggered their curiosity about taking the vaccine. Dr. Campbell took approximately twenty minutes to activate the drones in the vicinity.

Meanwhile, Linette observed her daughter trying to find ways to talk to Noah. Even though she was quite impressed with her skills, she was her daughter and felt the need to stop their conversation before it became too personal.

'Oh, I have a tattoo that no one in my family—' Samantha didn't notice she was being overheard by her mother.

'Alright!' Linette interrupted. 'Samantha, honey, go get your brother some food and we're going to talk about that tattoo once we get home.' She forced a smile and watched her daughter stomp off. She looked at Noah's nervous face and patted him on his shoulder before walking away.

The drones were ready to go airborne. 'Enter location.' The device displayed these words in a bold font. Dr. Campbell entered his address without hesitation and waited for it to calculate the best route. The device blacked out and a radar started fading in as small red dots, indicating the active drones, appeared. A loud high-pitched sound was heard—it was music to his ears. 'Forty-two drones, activated,' the device displayed. Raghav rubbed his hands against each other and laid back with dignity.

'Not everyone listens to the radio,' Noah commented.

'These drones were displayed for a reason,' said Eric as he continued. 'One of the first devices to carry out all functions at once—from video to audio.'

'They have a speaker installed.'

'We will make the people listen to the radio through these drones.'

Dr. Campbell nodded his head at their discovery. 'Long before you two were playing Sherlock Holmes, I connected the radio to the drones, filled them with baskets of nasal sprays and they're already taking off.'

An army of drones took over the sky, and the voice of RJ Millie Wilson took over the sound of the propeller blades. The announcement on the streets from the skies went something like, 'Dear Annapolis, attention here. The vaccine for the ongoing virus outbreak has been found. This drone carries the vaccine. One person, one shot up your nose. It is a simple procedure and the only way to stop this virus from taking over.'

'All I have to do now is allot a house to each drone and then prepare a track for them that they would obey,' Dr. Campbell announced, watching the room lose interest in his boasting nature. He looked around for validation or something as dramatic as an applaud but no one showed engrossment.

However, the entire neighborhood admired the drones-filled sky. It felt as if an electronic sheet had taken over the sharp rays. People believed in their message.

Noah looked outside the window, glancing innocently until he heard these words from his father. 'Noah, get away from there.'

Yet another man, not dressed up as if he was in the previous gang, slowly opened the door as he watched Noah taking a few steps back.

Linette and Elora pulled Nathan and Arabella inside a room to keep their innocent eyes away from what was going to happen.

This man was not angry as the others, he was crying uncontrollably. His quivering mouth started speaking, 'I can't control it. Please end this pain.' He fell to his knees and held his head while sobbing. He was the first one who tried his best to control the malignant virus.

The environment was quiet, only the man's agony was heard. As for the others, a few tears did roll down, out of sympathy. None of them tried going near him, a single move would set him off to hurt someone, it could have triggered the virus.

Gracy pulled out her gun, pointing it at the man. She felt hesitant as she did the first time when she had to pull the trigger on an innocent man. Her guts stopped her from doing so yet again. She looked at Erica who had a calculating face on. 'What?' she whispered.

Erica nodded and whispered back, overtaking the man's cry, 'Looking at his wound, I can assure you that no one has gone this far without letting the virus take over. His immune system is brilliant. We can save—try to save him.' Her eyes moved to the very last dose of the vaccine they had, 'Doc,' she looked at Dr. Campbell, 'More than a thousand vaccines and this one is the last before you create more. You don't need it, do you?'

'Not more than he does,' he replied back.

Eric moved swiftly and grabbed the shot before Erica could get to it. She nodded her head but felt protected.

He slowly walked toward the man, feeling his heart rate increase with every step taken closer to him. The man fought for his breath and he had to be taken out of it immediately. Gracy prepared her gun, just in case of a surprise attack. Eric took a long breath and knelt down to level herself with the man. His body was steady as he put his hand forward to spray the vaccine up his nose.

At once, with a sudden gesture, Eric held the man's head and gave him the shot. He stood there, staring at the man as the crying soul seized right before his eyes.

His trembling body came to a sudden stop as the man coughed out chunks of blood. He felt a heavy pain in his chest; however, felt relieved as he finally had full control over his brain. He looked at the scared faces across the room and asked with a wheezing voice, 'What the hell was that?'

Erica subtly smiled and was impressed with how he fought the virus.

'That's creepy, why are you smiling like that?' asked the confused man, holding his heavy head.

Linette recognized his voice and rushed outside the room. 'Zander?' She frowned.

He picked himself up from the ground and sensed safety after looking at a familiar face. 'Linette!' Zander exclaimed. 'Linette, why do I know your name?'

'We're neighbors'

'Right! We're neighbors.' Zander seemed lost. 'How did I get here?'

'You were infected.'

'With what?'

'Where's Carrie?'

'Huh?' Zander could not pay attention to her words.

'Zander, where is your wife?'

'I—oh no, I don't, I don't remember! The last time I saw her, we were at home. I don't remember anything after that. Linette, where is my wife?!' He panicked.

'I don't—'

Jacob jumped into the conversation. 'I'll drive you to your place, we'll look for her.'

'Yeah that's—thank you whoever you are.' Zander tried to recall the past few hours. They both stepped outside, carefully watching their step as tiredness took over. 'What did I miss?' he asked Jacob as they sat inside the police car.

'A lot,' he replied as the engine sputtered.

'You're a cop. It's really kind of you to help me out. I always criticized our police depar—'

'Yeah, I needed a reason to get out of that house.'

'Alright then, just as I started appreciating—'

'Between you and me I killed an officer. I didn't kill her but I was the reason she left the house. I got a message saying that they found her. Something did seem odd about that message but I ignored it. Just a couple of minutes ago I read their entire message, they meant they found her body.' Jacob almost had tears in his eyes as he tried to concentrate on the road.

'Why are you telling me all this?' Zander tried processing.

'Yolanda Sophia Aguero was her name. She was a good one.'

'Why are you telling me all this?' he repeated, slowly this time. 'Cause you're a stranger and it looks like you're going to forget about what I said in a few hours.'

Chapter 23: Wait

Waiting is the worst part of every event. Be it waiting for the bride to arrive, waiting for your food at the restaurant, or waiting for a virus to pass. It's not easy for a city to recover from a massacre.

The city was heedful of what was happening. Officers were alerted. Annapolis was all over the news, and the media was back on the air, covering every bit of the vaccination process; however, they were still looking for the source of this rescue mission.

The last batch of the drones was sent out to finish off their job saving the city.

'It's been almost three hours, the batteries did not run out?' Samantha questioned.

'My device runs for five hours keeping the drones charged till they're connected,' Raghav replied, moderately tired of answering questions.

'How is that possible?'

'Um Science.'

'Are we sure that the cities nearby do not need any of these?' Gracy asked Eric.

'Well, they were on a lock down—'

'After days.'

'We don't have enough vaccines.'

'Maybe we should.'

'Hopefully not.'

Noah interrupted their quarrel, 'I have friends in the nearby cities and they confirmed there was nothing barbaric going on there, the authorities have it under control.'

Eric raised his eyebrows at Gracy. She scoffed and looked away.

'Where's the president?' Dr. Cambell nodded.

'We don't talk about that.' Eric sighed.

Meanwhile, Linette felt as if she had been forgetting something, and then after a while, it hit her. 'I am so absent-minded! Samantha, where is Aunt Evelyn? What are you guys doing here?'

'Evelyn's a Zombie,' Samantha stated, quite confidently.

'She's a what?' Linette tried processing her blunt sentence.

'She might be infected,' Raghav added. 'There are a couple of people who did not attend to the drone, she was one of them. I've written down these house numbers and will need some of you to check them out.'

'We'll go,' Alexis and Zachery announced in unison.

'How many?' Marcos asked.

'Six.'

'That's a fair number,' Alexis joined in. 'Give us the list, we four can go check these out.' He looked at Poppy and Zachery while signaling them to agree; so they did.

As all four officers stepped outside in a rush, Alexis told them about Sophia's death, leaving them dismayed.

'Does Gracy know?' Poppy questioned.

'I highly doubt that. We should keep it that way until things quiet down a bit,' Alexis replied.

'That's only gonna get her more furious,' Zachery added.

'Sophia was under Gracy's team, we have to tell her sometime soon,' said Poppy.

'Poppy's right, but for now, let's check out those houses and get it over with,' said Marcos as everyone acceded.

It's midnight, the four houses were empty, one house took a lot of convincing to take the unauthorized vaccine, and the sixth house—Evelyn's—she was infected. However, Poppy was brave enough to save her by shooting the vaccine up the infected's nose. After a little reluctance, she was put to rest. Making sure it was safe to be around the woman, Poppy notified Linette as she landed up at Evelyn's with her kids.

The team left for Zachery's apartment to discuss Sophia. 'What about her parents? Did someone notify them?' Poppy asked.

'Woman, she left back no information for us,' Alexis replied.

'As far as I know Jacob, he's blaming himself for this and has probably resigned.'

At Dr. Campbell's.

'We're going to take a leave. Anything else we can help you with?' Eric asked Dr. Campbell.

'Wait. All we can do now is wait,' he replied.

'I almost forgot Katherine Collins called. She wanted in on the vaccine and welcomed us to open a vaccination drive at her center. Looks like we have people on our side, we could really use it, you know?'

'Eric, you very well know I work alone.'

'For yourself, yes. We're talking about saving a city here. She's also a virologist, and probably has more information than you.'

'I will speak to Katherine.'

Eric nodded a yes as they firmly shook hands. He took off with Gracy and Erica, back to Gracy's house—where his parents were recovering their energy.

Dr. Campbell was left alone in the living room, as he stared at the broken door. He sighed in frustration and tried fixing the hinges of the door. His eyes moved to the sample vaccine. Nothing was over for him, his role in this epidemic had just begun—meeting with the health authorities, and the recreation of the vaccine while making sure that the virus does not develop and become stronger than it already is. Collaborating with Katherine Collins—not a very appealing fact for him; however, he's doing it for his city and if things got worse, for his country.

At Annapolis.

The Fenjaitus had taken over the city. Only time would tell them if the vaccines worked if the place was virus-free if there was anything to worry about anymore. The most restless part had arrived—all they had to do was wait.

Chapter 24: Heroes

Do heroes like the label they've been given? Sure, a compliment doesn't hurt but to be called a hero? Sounds a tad bit dramatic, doesn't it? 'You're my hero!' You might like being called a hero but some feel pressured, as if they are now responsible for taking every matter into their own hands, some just can't deal with that word.

In a week's time, completely infected ones were hunted down, and the vaccine gained fame and got approved by the health authorities—with a small price to pay for not notifying them before—and finally, the city was back to its old self. The authorities ensured that it was the day of celebration with absolutely zero cases—no sign of destruction. With a few more days passing by and being completely sure of the situation, they declared Annapolis a Zermaitus-free city.

It was a golden hour, nature seemed pleasant and beautiful as it tried to recover from the misery it had gone through. People felt safe again; there was a sense of relief in the air. Some stepped out of their homes to greet their neighbors whereas the others waited for their loved ones to return. However, they were long gone. The bodies were collected and kept at Collins' Research Center. Some of them had name tags, while the others were just unidentified corpses due to their destroyed faces.

The news, the radio, and every media outlet had been talking about only one group and how they dramatically saved the city in not more than three months. Over the radio, RJ Millie Wilson finally got the chance to interview Gracy and Eric.

'This virus seemed obstinate till you guys introduced us to the antidote in a rather unimaginable way. So tell our listeners, how does it feel to save the city to be called the heroes of Annapolis?

'It's flattering but I don't think we should be called that.' Eric nodded as he was not proud of what had happened. 'We sure did help everyone out with the vaccine but we didn't save the city, ma'am. There were a lot of people who died. We lost a lot of loved ones to the virus. We are barely a bunch of heroes. There were people out there with big plans who couldn't make it.'

'People who deserved to live. We did not save the city,' Gracy added. 'The virus is still out there, we didn't put a stop to it. It's going to be among us as the normal flu but it can develop. It's hardly a heroic moment for any of us, we'll be witnessing a lot of funerals and it won't be easy.'

'It was, no doubt, an unfortunate event. Some people couldn't be saved but the city was surely saved. And there's mourning, I've heard?' Millie tried covering up.

'Yes.' Eric played along with the change of topic. 'Tomorrow afternoon at Quiet Waters Park. We'll be paying our respect to those who couldn't make it.'

'That is a beautiful gesture. Eric, have you lost anyone who was close to you? Did it affect you in the process of saving—I mean in your work,' Millie asked, hesitantly.

He looked at Millie and took a deep breath. He clearly mentioned a formal interview. However, Millie made a sympathetic face and pleaded with him to continue.

'I did.' Eric moved further away from the mic. 'Maverick and Hendricks. They were also helping us out with getting the vaccine.' He emotionlessly nodded at Millie.

Noticing Eric's stutter, Millie knew it was wrong of her to bring that up. 'My condolences to you and to everyone who lost their loved ones. As of now, the city cannot thank you and your team enough. Would you care to share at least a gist of how you managed to find a cure to a deadly virus?'

'We'd rather not get into details with that,' Gracy replied. 'Some things are better hidden in shadows. It sounds disbelieving but this virus entered the city from an island, we traveled back there to get the vaccine'

'We're waiting to hear more'

Eric rolled his eyes and added, 'It's going to be all over the news, no matter how much we hide the story. So, you'll get your information from there.'

'Oh, alright! Would you like to convey anything to our listeners before we end this interview?'

'I do.' Eric sat up straight. 'We haven't defeated this virus, it's the strongest thing we're fighting against and we will be needing stronger doses to overcome it. Don't live in fear, that's not what I'm saying. I'm only trying to prepare—'

'Thank you!' Millie interrupted. 'It was great having you two on The Morning Show Blow! This city has been saved by the heroes of Annapolis and hopefully, we'll be interviewing more such brilliant minds. Till then, signing out, RJ Millie Wilson!' Millie cued a soft melody and slammed her headphones against the counter.

'Why did you cut me off?' Eric was furious.

'My listeners need soft words right now, not another stress!' she yelled back.

'But that was the truth, they need to know that this is not over. And you can't label us as heroes!' Gracy joined the argument.

'You both just ruined my stress-free show,' said Millie.

'And what about the stress you were drowning us in? Have a heart, we do not want to talk about our personal lives here in front of the whole city.' Eric tried keeping himself calm.

'You were my friend and we trusted you to do this without making it sound like a fairy tale. Thanks for all your help, but none of my team members will be interviewing here with you,' said Gracy, and they both left the studio.

'I'm sorry for dragging you into this,' said Gracy to Eric as her voice frequency fluctuated due to climbing down the stairs.

'We're not heroes,' said Eric as he unlocked his Ford Fusion.

Gracy nodded and hopped into the car.

Eric rested his hands on the steering wheel and shook the drama off his shoulders. He accelerated and went back home as they watched the cheerful streets, rejoicing.

At Linette's.

Linette sobbed by the window in solitary. Her tears were for Hunter, her sorrow for Aaron. Her apologies to both of the men remained untold. Linette found herself in a dilemma. It was either telling Samantha the entire story or pretending as if Hunter never existed.

After putting a lot of thought into it, she decided to start the former by placing their childhood picture beside a family frame. It threw her back to the time when they were only ten years old. The moment was captured in front of a roller coaster. Their arms were wrapped around each other as if they had nothing to worry about.

'Is that Dad?' asked a voice from behind. 'I didn't know you guys were childhood friends.'

Linette got startled as she gasped. 'Oh, Samantha.' She pressed her lips. 'He is your father, but not the father you've known for years.'

Samantha scoffed. 'What do you mean?'

'Sit with me.' She lent her a glass of water—Samantha could either drink the water or throw the glass—either way could be comforting. 'You've met this man before, just not the way you should have and I am to be blamed for it. I need you to prepare yourself and listen carefully because what I'm about to tell you can take unexpected paths.'

At Roger's.

He sat down on the carpet with his briefcase. His eyes were fixed on his partially shattered window. His blurry vision shifted from the crack to his briefcase. His lips twitched as he tried smiling at his favorite possession. He reached out to his pocket to remove a hip flask, preparing himself for a mental breakdown. He placed the stainless steel, filled with strong intoxication, aside.

He gathered some courage and unlocked his briefcase. The first thing that caught his attention was a matte black watch. He stared at the ticking hand clock as it took him back to an old yet fresh memory from two years ago.

'Guys this looks expensive! You didn't have to go all out.' Roger grinned.

'Sure, give it back then. I'll sell this and get a better engagement ring for my girl,' Gale put his hand forward.

'Or we could just give it to Stefano,' said Adrian.

'Oh yeah Promotion!!!' Evan announced.

'Roger, keep it brother. Before we change our minds and actually take it back.' Aaron folded his hands.

'Plus this is the only expensive shit I'll get from you guys,' Roger mocked as they all laughed in agreement.

Roger smiled as his eyes turned red. He felt the need to open his flask and take a sip of the burning liquid but he resisted.

He kept the hand clock aside and removed a group polaroid.

'Alright, boys! Just one picture, don't talk, don't blink, don't breathe,' Martha exaggerated.

'Geez, Martha' Akshay mumbled.

'Say cheese!' William said in a high-pitched voice.

'Shut up, Willy!' everyone yelled in unison as they heard a click.

'What? No! We weren't ready!' Jack exclaimed.

'Here take the polaroid. Sometimes impromptu images gather more memories than the planned ones.'

Roger sobbed. He wiped off a chunk of sticky mucus that ran from his cold red nose. His mind—still deciding whether to intake the liquor or not. He placed the neat polaroid back inside the briefcase, carefully.

He took out a cassette recorder. It was the recording of their first research. He switched it on and prepared himself to hear their voices.

'How to start this thing?' Evan asked.

'It's on, I gave it to you that way.' Aaron sighed.

'Wait I know how to use this um, how do I stop this?'

'What was the boss thinking when he made us a team?' Gale scoffed.

'Guys, we should try and accommodate with what we have,' said Aaron.

'What we have is a researcher who does not know how to use a fuc—'

Roger switched off the device and looked up as he tried breathing through his mouth. Tears ran down his cheeks as he finally reached out to his flask and emptied it at once. The burning liquid could not hurt him, he was hurt enough. It was too soon for him to relive those old memories. He sat there, motionless, wondering how he ended up there all alone.

At Gracy's.

The house kept itself entertained with the news. 'Mister Stefano Alfred has been sued by the families of the researchers who were assigned the island project. Here are some clips of Mister Stefano defending himself,' said a reporter as the screen switched to another footage.

'It was my loss too!' Stefano yelled. 'I lost some best reporters! They just need to blame someone! This is injustice!'

'Due to violent graphics, the whole video cannot be shown—'

'No fun, they should stop censoring violence,' said Emanuel as he switched off the television.

'Oh, the Aristarchus blood never leaves.' Erica pressed her lips as they chuckled.

'What now?' Eric asked.

'Unfortunately, we are heading back. The lockdown has been lifted and your mother and I have to go back to work,' Emanuel replied.

'Are you sure you won't be needing some time to—'

'Hey, Aristarchus blood, right? We don't need time to process anything,' said Abiyeth. 'And we'll be taking Erica with us.'

'It's important I explore the real world and do something for myself,' said Erica, maturely.

Eric seemed impressed with her meaningful decisions. 'We will finally have the house to ourselves,' he whispered to Gracy as they silently chuckled.

Gracy looked at him from the corner of her eyes and took a sigh of relief, leaving behind the horrors of Fenjiyawa.

At Jacob's.

He was drowning too but in chip crumbs. As Poppy had predicted, he did hand over his resignation to the department, and ever since that day, he did not leave his couch. He munched on various snacks and binge-watched loads of movies. Jacob had no intention of moving his arse until he heard a knock on his door.

'Just leave the pizza at the door!' Jacob assumed while surfing through the channels.

'Um it's not the pizza guy,' Poppy replied from the other side.

Jacob's body bolted upright as he heard her voice. He looked around and prepared himself to face embarrassment. He kept the packet of chips on the coffee table and wiped off his cheese-filled hands on the couch. Jacob picked himself up and dragged his lazy soul to open the door. He witnessed a woman dressed in a red gown standing behind a bouquet of flowers that complemented her dress.

'Jacob! How are you?' The tone of excitement in her voice got minimized as she saw Jacob's unshaved face and god-awful attire. She peeked inside and sighted leftover snacks all over the house, half-eaten sandwiches, and crushed packets of chips on all the seating furniture.

Howls from a speeding 1968 black Mustang caught their attention and made them turn toward it.

'Am I day dreaming or were they' Jacob squinted.

'Marcos and Alexis? They are,' Poppy replied. 'We all got promoted and a pretty high raise, so they rented that for today's event.'

'Event?'

'The department, before mourning our officers' death, decided to host an event for us to just—it's a get together where we not like a get-together but—'

'It's fine, I get it.'

'Thank you can I come in?'

'Of course!' He made way for her to enter.

She looked around and scoffed. 'Wow.'

'I'm sorry, Poppy. Had I known you were going to stop by, I would have cleaned up.' He felt his uneven beard and stood there, humiliated.

'Oh, no. This place looks exactly like mine.'

'O OK?' Jacob pressed his lips as his eyes wandered.

'Thank you for what you did on the ship. You stood in front of me, the arrow could've gotten you.'

'You don't have to thank me for that.' He gulped as he felt awkwardness slowly taking over.

'And sorry about that day I yelled at you.'

'You yelled at me every day.'

'Sorry for all those days,' she corrected herself.

'It's OK.' He nodded and looked down.

She kept the bouquet on his couch and delicately walked toward the door as her heels tapped against the crispy floor. 'There's something I have to—'

'I'm sorry you had to see this side of me,' Jacob interrupted, hesitantly.

'Sorry for what? You eat junk over getting drunk, that's weirdly adorable.'

They chortled for a while and quieted down again. The awkwardness between them started disappearing for good.

Their moment was interrupted by screeching wheels. 'Get a room!' Alexis yelled.

'Hop in, both of you!' Marcos added.

'Me too?' Jacob stepped back in astonishment.

'We're here to tell you that we got you your job back.' She handed him his application letter to re-apply for the same position that he had left behind. 'The punishment for quitting this way is that you won't be getting promoted.'

Jacob's jaw dropped as he grabbed the paper from her hand. 'This is perfect! You have no idea how much I regretted leaving that sweet uniform!'

'I know.' Poppy smiled. 'You need to clean yourself up and get in your tux.'

He leaned over and gently kissed her cheeks. 'Officers!' He called out the men as he pointed them out. Poppy pressed her lips and blushed unmanageably as she watched him rush inside and come back out as a worthy officer.

At Raghav's.

The family settled on the white dining table for a feast. The aroma of Elora's freshly cooked turkey took over the entire floor. She drizzled leafy herbs on the turkey with her tender fingers. She poured the Sangiovese wine for Raghav and herself as the soft liquid touched the bottom of the wine glass, whereas the children got cranberry juice.

Raghav unfolded the white linen napkin and carefully placed it on his lap, while the others did not bother to make this sophisticated move. He looked at them with disappointment, wondering if they would ever learn the basic table manners or not. However, his thoughts were disturbed by Noah's out-of-the-blue topic.

'Malignance,' Noah declared out loudly, with pride.

'What?' Elora frowned.

'What are you talking about?' Dr. Campbell squinted his eyes, watching Noah glance at a loose paper.

'We got an email from our literature professor. She asked us to write down a poem related to this unexpected massacre we experienced. Thought a lot and came up with the name Malignance, meaning horror and chaos or whatever. The class is gonna flip!' Noah jumped in excitement.

'I see this virus is giving your professors an easy way out with the homework.' Raghav sat back and crossed his arms. 'I like the name.'

'Read it to us.' Elora smiled at him.

Noah cleared his throat and continued, 'Malignance.' He stopped proudly and looked around at curious faces. 'That's pretty much all I got.'

'Oh.' Elora raised her eyebrows and continued serving food to herself.

They all sat upright to proceed with their supper. The clashes of cutleries and slurps had slowly taken over the quiet atmosphere. After a long moment of silence, Noah started another conversation.

'So, Father—'

'Yes, Son?' Dr. Campbell looked at Noah with a rare smile.

'Have you.' Noah's voice took a high-pitched tone. 'Have you ever tried switching on my drone with your device? Because a few times I did feel that my drone was acting weird.'

'I haven't seen much.'

'Great. Perfect.'

'But I'd say it's rather childish to put up my wife's picture on your dart board and recklessly aim for her eyes.'

'Noah!' Elora exclaimed as she watched him choke on his drink. He wiped off the splashed liquid from his chin and raised his eyebrows, preparing to give a damn good explanation. However, laughter broke out. A delightful environment surely took over as Noah chuckled nervously.

Amidst this happiness, a simple house fly had made its way to a pile of cupcakes. House flies. As harmless as they sound, as lightly as people take them, they could ruin a person's life with one contact. The fly was not alone. It had traveled from the exposed morgue, with fresh infected blood. Leaving every single particle of it on the cupcake, it flew away as Raghav's hungry hand reached out for that particular piece.

'Dessert before supper? Who are you?' Elora threw her suspicious looks at him.

'I feel content.' He smiled at her. 'Which is why.' His eyes moved to Noah. 'I will consider buying you that game you wanted for months now. The last of us, was it?'

'Y-yeah.' Noah replied as he tried to bottle up his excitement.

'You've been obsessing over that game forever, what is it even about?'

'Zombies.' Noah pressed his lips and frowned while looking down at his delicious platter.

'Zombies.' He sighed and nodded his head in despair. He examined the chocolate cupcake as his saliva kept producing itself in his mouth. Unaware of the infected blood drops that were absorbed by the cake, he took a bite out of the overwhelming flavored bread as he murmured underneath his mouth-watering breath, 'Scrumptious.'